CARCHARODON

PAUL CARBERRY

CARCHARODON

PAUL CARBERRY

ENGEN
BOOKS

Published in Canada by Engen Books, St. John's, NL.

Library and Archives Canada Cataloguing in Publication

Title: Carcharodon / Paul Carberry.
Names: Carberry, Paul, 1984- author.
Identifiers: Canadiana (print) 20200333534 | Canadiana (ebook) 20200333550 |
ISBN 9781989473801
  (softcover) | ISBN 9781989473818 (PDF)
Classification: LCC PS8605.A6843 C37 2020 | DDC C813/.6—dc23

Distributed by:
Engen Books
www.engenbooks.com
submissions@engenbooks.com

First mass market paperback printing: October 2020

Cover Image: Shutterstock
Cover Design: Ellen Curtis

For Mom and Dad,
For introducing me to the joy of reading

CHAPTER ONE

The **Swift Current**
Near the Grand Banks
Off the Coast of Southern Newfoundland

The waves lapped off the side of the *Swift Current*. Each wave sounded like wet feet slapping against the surface. Jonah McGilvery tried to hold his hand steady, the cloudy liquid splashing over the rim of his cup. He cursed each wave as it jolted his yacht back and forth. A strong southerly gust carrying the unseasonably warm air from Maine over the icy Labrador Current formed a dense layer of fog that had sneaked in. Jonah was too drunk to acknowledge the sudden transition in the weather. The *Swift Current* sank further into the swell of the water as the tide began to surge. Disappearing behind a wall of fog, the coast hid beneath the mysterious midnight sky as the clouds masked the moonlight. White tips at the ridge of each wave were the only reference points Jonah could see as they rolled towards him.

Jonah fetched himself one more drink before heading back to the St. John's port. His company, Labyrinth Oil, had persuaded the federal government to sell him the rights to St. John's Harbour. Several factors had stumbled into place for him that favored the sale. Global warming had started to affect the island of Newfoundland; you could see the drastic changes in the ocean's erratic currents just off its shorelines. The waters surrounding the island had become unpredictable, making it too treacherous for any fisherman to make a living. The decline of the fisheries meant less money for the government, and the economy of St. John's had taken a hard hit. Labyrinth Oil developed a technique allowing them to extract the rich oil deposits deep underneath the turbulent currents of the Grand Banks without having to build an offshore oil rig. This would help generate jobs for the laid off fishermen who had become desperate for work.

Jonah stumbled down the ladder leading to the cabin of the *Swift Current* and nearly toppled over backwards as the ship sank deep into the trough of the rising waves. Jonah clutched the rail and waited until his legs got used to the swells underneath him. His bottle of dark spiced rum rested in a wine holder affixed to the marble counter. He was glad that the large waves hadn't knocked it loose. "One more drink," Jonah lied to himself as he stumbled forwards.

A loud crash rocked the *Swift Current* violently. Jonah lost his balance and crashed hard, face first, into the wooden bar. The glass flew from his hand and smashed against the hardwood boards sending sharp shards of glass scattering across the floor of the galley. A piece of his tooth cracked off, scattering across the bar counter. The room spun around in Jonah's blurred view; the warm, sticky tang of blood filled his mouth as his upper tooth bit though his cheek. He could feel the boat rise and fall with the waves, but somehow the boat was being held in place. Waves crashed over the yacht in a deafening rumble, and water cascaded down the companion ladder in rhythmic spurts.

Jonah figured the waves must have drifted the *Swift Current* against some rugged rocks. He reached up and grasped the forty-ounce bottle, taking a generous swig of rum. It burned as it rushed down his throat and splashed into his empty belly. Jonah walked back to the ladder and got a mouthful of saltwater as another wave crashed over the yacht. He stuck his head out of the hole just in time to watch the next wave roll over the deck. The force of the wave nearly knocked him back down, but he managed to hold on long enough for it to pass over. He pulled himself onto the deck and grabbed hold of the wheel, bracing himself against the crashing wave. There was complete darkness above and below, the fog making it near impossible to see the root of the problem. He took another long gulp from the bottle, wiping his lips with his wet sleeve leaving behind the bitter brine of saltwater.

He turned the ignition of the *Swift Current*, and the diesel engine roared to life as he pushed the throttle forward. The engine howled loudly, but the yacht remained arrested in place; a thick plume of smoke billowed from below. "Curse it," Jonah swore again as he eased back on the throttle. Another wave roared over the yacht and knocked Jonah off his feet, and he slid across the slick deck. His leg smashed hard into the metal railing, and an excruciating pain radiated from his thigh as his femur splintered into pieces. The *Swift Current* bobbed up and down in the raging waves, water crashing over Jonah making it hard to breathe. He reached back and tried to pull himself away from the railing, but his hands slipped in something oily. He glanced over his shoulder, and a chill shot down his spine. A giant tentacle full of suckers ran over the deck and down the side of the yacht. It must have been roughly twenty-feet long and nearly a foot thick. The massive tentacle of *Architeuthis dux* had been holding the *Swift Current* in place.

"Jesus Christ." Jonah tried to stand up, but the pain in his leg was overwhelming. He fell flat on the deck, dragging himself towards the steering column. The boat began to rise with the tide, but the giant squid held the stern of the vessel in place. Jonah reached out for anything to stop himself from slipping. Another wave crashed down on him. The force sent him hurtling towards the colossal squid, its shiny white beak waiting for him. "Help!" Jonah screamed out in vain. He was all alone in the vast ocean with no one around him for miles, the weather much too treacherous for anyone to venture out in. A giant, soulless eye stared back at him from the large pink body. Jonah could see only a sliver of light in its large black pupil. He closed his eyes and braced himself against the jagged beak of the *Architeuthis*.

A loud splash boomed over the thunderous roar of the waves, and a spray of thick slime washed over Jonah. He opened his eyes to find complete darkness over the edge of his yacht. The giant tentacle remained stuck to the deck of the *Swift Current*; everything else torn away. A dark slick covered Jonah's face and mixed with the water on the deck. The boat drifted with the waves now, but somehow the starboard side of the yacht turned towards the waves. Jonah looked on in horror as a giant wall of darkness towered over him. The wave pounded the *Swift Current* and sent him tumbling into the water.

As Jonah plunged into the icy cold waters, his muscles seized solid with shock. He screamed; air bubbles escaped his mouth, dancing around his face. He didn't recognize which way was up, water covering him like a black sheet pulled over his eyes. Jonah kicked his legs and thrashed his arms once the shock wore off, not knowing which direction the surface was. Darkness shrouded him.

Something powerful snapped closed over his chest, driving the remaining oxygen from his lungs. Razor-sharp teeth pierced his flesh, shredding the soft meat with ease. Jonah felt blood pumping out of his body through the jagged wounds. He peered down and came eye to eye with the cold dead eyes of his maker. With a brutal jerk of its body, the *Carcharodon carcharias* tore hunks of flesh from its prey, its jaw jutting forward to get a stronger grasp on the carcass in its mouth. The juice from the giant *Architeuthis* had sent the giant great white into a frenzied state. It devoured Jonah whole within a matter of minutes. This creature stalked the ocean for forty years now, and five years ago it was driven into the deepest parts of the ocean by orcas and over fishing. The frigid cold waters of the ocean had altered this shark into sizes not seen by humans before. Lateral lines, tubes that ran along the enormous creature's body, filled with fluids that helped it sense vibrations in any direction. These lines began just under the creature's snout and ran down the sides of its body, helping it to track down its prey. With every movement of its body, the muscles enveloping the canals warmed the fluids inside, allowing the shark to stay warm in the frosty depths of the ocean. Thirty feet long, weighing close to eight-thousand pounds, it wasn't the only great white shark cruising the Grand Banks of Newfoundland.

CHAPTER TWO

Newfoundland and Labrador

Five-hundred million years ago a warm equatorial water mass called the Iapetus Ocean covered the land mass that would form Newfoundland. The continents of Europe, Africa, and North America surrounded the Iapetus Ocean. Over the next one-hundred million years these continents drifted towards each other on a collision course by forces deep within the earth's mantle. This collision smashed the ocean floor into jagged rock formation, thrusting up huge land masses to establish the Appalachian mountain chain. We find this mountain chain throughout the British Isles and all the way to Norway. Once this tremendous collision ended four-hundred million years ago, it formed one giant land mass called Pangaea.

Then, 225 million years ago, the same forces that set the continents on a collision course ripped them apart. This left a piece of Africa on Signal Hill in St. John's, North America's oldest city. As the continents drifted apart, it created a large gap which filled with water, forming the Atlantic Ocean. Then, during the ice age, gargantuan glaciers formed across the earth. Once these giant, frozen

masses of ice melted, they carved the landscape of the island that the people of Newfoundland call home. These
sheets of ice reached upwards of a kilometre in thickness
and carved the land to form lakes and cut deep enough to
form rivers and lakes. Bays located on the western coast of
Newfoundland resemble the fjords in Norway.

Over hundreds of millions of years, different species
roamed the earth. Dinosaurs roamed across the land that
is now Newfoundland during the Jurassic and Cretaceous
period. Abundant aquatic life-forms filled the waters surrounding Newfoundland. The codfish, so plentiful, could
block the passage of European ships. Seal hunting off the
coast of Labrador had once been a thriving industry but
now faltered because of different animal rights activists.
Casting a bloody image over the industry, it soon faltered. Even the whale hunting industry boomed during
the twentieth century.

Newfoundlanders have suffered over the last century.
The people living here have seen great tragedies befall the
citizens in unimaginable disasters. The sealing disaster of
1914 was the start of a long list of tragedies that shaped
the harsh way of life in Newfoundland during the last
century. During a wicked storm on the ice flows on March
30, 1914, the crew of the S.S. *Newfoundland* and the S.S.
Stephano returned to the ice. They left to kill seals, despite
the signs of worsening weather. Both captains thought the
sealers were safely aboard the other vessel. The sealers,
caught in the freezing rain and darkness, endured a night
without shelter. Then, still soaking wet from the night
before, a snow storm struck the next day. Only fifty-four
men out of the 132 sealers survived the forty-eight-hour

ordeal from hell. Captain Isaac Randell of the S.S. *Bellaventure* rescued them from their horrible fate. The survivors suffered life changing injuries from the extreme frostbite. Many sealers had lost limbs and fingers. This same storm claimed the lives of the entire crew of the S.S. *Southern Cross*. While official marine court of inquiry determined that the ship sank in the same blizzard, they could not find evidence to verify this. People believe greedy owners allowed the *Southern Cross* to sail with rotten boards, which succumbed to the pressures of the heavy sea. The storm took the lives of over 250 men from the three sealing ships, a collective tragedy known as the 1914 Newfoundland Sealing Disaster.

On the Burin Peninsula in November, 1929, a tsunami carrying giant waves at forty kilometers an hour pounded the shores. It washed entire homes from dozens of communities out to the sea, killing twenty-eight people and leaving hundreds more homeless. This destructive force of nature only compounded the economy of Newfoundland and Labrador during a worldwide depression. Back in 1929, the country didn't own a seismograph or tide gauge. This device could have warned the residents of the island the tsunami was approaching after an earthquake rattled the Grand Banks, registering a 7.2 on the Richter scale. At 7:30 pm on the eighteenth of November, residents along the Burin Peninsula noticed a severe and rapid drop in sea level. Unknown to residents, this was moments before the trough of the tsunami's first wave stuck. Portions of the ocean floor that had remained submerged for years was now exposed. This sudden drop in water levels caused docked boats to tumbled over onto their sides. Then just minutes later, three successive waves hammered the shores, flooding the coastline and raising the water up to twenty-three feet above normal. The swell in the peninsula's long narrow bays caused the water to rise as high as eighty-eight feet. There was no refuge that night, the storm only a fraction of the ocean's wrath that day. In only thirty minutes powerful waves ripped homes from their foundation. Motor boats and schooners swept out to the sea. The enormous force destroyed wharves and fish plants. Thousands of pounds of salt cod washed back into the ocean. In another cruel twist of fate, a snow storm damaging the telegraph wire isolated the entire peninsula from the rest of the world. It was not until three days afterward that the outside world learned of the fate of the Burin Peninsula.

A German submarine attacked the S.S. *Caribou* during the Battle of the St. Lawrence by a German U-boat on the night of October thirteenth in 1942. The night was pitch black with no moon. Under the command of Ulrich Graf, U-69 spotted the *Caribou* belching heavy smoke off the coast of Newfoundland. At 3:40 am, confusing the *Caribou* for a two-stack destroyer, Graf sent a lone torpedo into the starboard side. The explosion caused mass chaos, and, in a sadistic twist of fate, several of the lifeboats were unable to launch or were destroyed. This forced many passengers to jump overboard into the bitter cold Atlantic waters. Out of the 230 people aboard the *Caribou, 136* perished.

On the fourteenth of February, 1982, the Ocean Ranger received reports of an approaching storm caused by a major Atlantic cyclone. Neighboring rigs had received reports of a broken port light and water in the ballast control room. Stormy seas of up to sixty-five feet with winds gusting at one-hundred knots pounded the Atlantic Ocean. At 0052 local time on the fifteenth of February, the Ocean Ranger sent out a call noting a severe list to the port side of the rig and called for immediate aid. During the night, the adverse winter storm sank the Ocean Ranger. A crew of eighty-four lost forever.

The ocean has played a huge role shaping the lives of Newfoundlanders. Waves eroded the rocky shorelines and claimed countless victims. With the effects of greenhouse gasses changing the world's climates and melting the ice caps, global warming will soon ravage the shores of Newfoundland and Labrador. The melting ice caps flood into the Labrador Current, carrying an influx of frigid water to the island of Newfoundland.

Bergmann's rule states that creatures with greater masses are better able to regulate their internal body temperature. Creatures who live in cold water will grow larger. Now with the waters off the coast of Newfoundland and Labrador colder than ever before, the creatures that inhabit the surrounding waters will increase in magnitude.

CHAPTER THREE

St. John's Harbour
Harbour Masters Quarters
Labyrinth Oil News Conference

The sun burned a golden yellow high in the sky, piercing through the haze of the mid-afternoon smog. Kevin O'Reilly remained in the cab of his old Dodge with the air conditioner turned up, staring at the temperature readout on the dash. Another sweltering day in the mid-thirties, an extraordinary occurrence for two straight weeks in September. This summer was the hottest on record, breaking last year's temperatures with ease. Global warming had wreaked havoc for years and there was nothing to be done about it.

Kevin parked outside of the Harbour Masters Quarters, expecting the news conference scheduled by Labyrinth Oil. He regularly discovered an excuse to escape home early. His marriage had been breaking down for years, and, with the increased pressure imposed on it, the less effort Kevin put into working on saving it. His wife, Amy, had tried desperately to conceive children, but the doctors had determined that he wasn't capable of reproducing. The marriage fell apart the day she told him she was pregnant; she claimed it was a miracle, but Kevin had his doubts. Rumors of his wife's unfaithful ways spread throughout town, making him a laughingstock. Paternity tests proved his doubts correct, but by that time he had grown to love the child as his own. Once his son had grown up and moved off to college, Kevin had no reason to stick around but he had lost his youthful good looks. His broad shoulders and muscular chest looked smaller now compared to his growing stomach. His hairline fading into a widow's peak with streaks of grey taking over his copper curls. People didn't look at him the same way anymore; girls no longer turned their heads when he walked into a bar. He generally spent too much time and money on an attractive lady at the bar before she left with a younger man. He yearned for those days.

An irate mob assembled outside in the parking lot, composed of two very distinct groups of protesters. Their common hatred united each with their own reasons to hate Labyrinth Oil. Burly fishermen comprised the first group, agitated by the blistering sun as they waited for the announcement. Even though everyone had known the rumors for months, people were still turning up expecting the crushing statement. Kevin had given up being a fisherman at an early age, instead choosing to work for the coast guard after struggling for years to make ends meet. The government had always kept the fishing industry in Newfoundland down even though everyone knew how bountiful the Flemish Cap was just off the southern coast. For hundreds of years until the cod moratorium in 1992, the Flemish Cap provided the fisherman of this province a living. For years other countries continued to reap the benefits of the fertile fishing grounds, while the hardworking people of this province had to stand by and watch.

It took years for the rights of the Grand Banks and Flemish Cap to be rewarded back to Canada and handed over to its rightful owners. Newfoundlanders were so close to bringing the fishing industry back to the top, but it happened about ten years too late. Labyrinth Oil had discovered an oil reserve so large they would stop at nothing to get their greedy hands on it. Their claim to fame was their revolutionary oil pumps that sucked the oil straight from the grounds off the coast of South Africa. The pipes contained suction pumps and motors within junctions every fifty metres, drawing the valuable fluids out with no oil rigs in the water. They had come under scrutiny from environmentalists who believed they altered whale migration routes, but they couldn't prove Labyrinth Oil had been directly involved. One thing was certain, the fishing industry in South Africa suffered when Labyrinth Oil placed their oil pipes.

The other half of the angry gathering were environmentalists, the brains to the fisherman's brawn. They were a mixture of university professors, students, and "hippies," as Kevin often said. Kevin didn't understand their plight. They weren't fighting for their jobs or money. They were fighting for the environment. Kevin looked around at their signs that read "Save the Whales," "Protect our Environment," and "Global Warming." They hollered out nonsense about how oil was ruining the planet. Kevin shook his head in disgust as he listened to their cries. Didn't they understand that the world ran on oil and without it they'd all be living in the dark ages?

It was time for the meeting to take place, but no one had walked onto the stage yet. Kevin grabbed a better view of the press conference. He turned off his truck and opened the door. A smothering heat smacked him in the face. Beads of sweat rolling down his back, Kevin thought about closing the door and cranking the air conditioning, but the electric crowd urged him closer. The angry grumbling and high-pitched fever that swept over the raucous assembly immediately infected Kevin, drawing him into the growing mob. Harbour security and the local law enforcement had assembled near the stage, working to keep matters under control.

"Get out here!"

"You're destroying our oceans!"

"Yellow-bellied coward!"

"Show yourself!"

"Trying to take away my livelihood!"

Men and women shouted at the empty stage, waiting impatiently for Jonah McGilvery to walk out of the Harbour Masters Quarters and onto the platform. "Where are you? You're a piece of shit!" Kevin screamed out, trying to push things further towards a confrontation. The crowd didn't need much of a push it seemed; it had been teetering on the brink of hysteria.

"You fucking prick!"

"I'll gut you!"

Police officers shouted out warnings to the mob, advocating for calmness. A wicked smile crossed Kevin's face as the officers' pleas fell on deaf ears. People hollered hateful threats at Jonah that fueled the crowd, each insult enticing another horrid remark.

The doors of the Harbour Masters Quarters opened, a hush fell over the parking lot as they waited for Jonah to show his face. A young Asian man dressed in a grey suit led the way. He slicked his short, dark hair back. A white dress shirt poked out beneath the grey tunic. His brown shoes shimmered in the sunlight. He was followed by a tall Asian woman in a maroon dress, her long black hair streaked with platinum blonde highlights. Her tanned skin caused the man to look pale in contrast. Her darkened features caught Kevin's attention. The door closed behind them without an appearance by the guest of honour, Jonah. They walked up the ramp, the woman's high-heeled stilettos clipping off the metal with each stride. Low rumbles and murmurs spread amongst the fishermen once again. They felt like Jonah had turned his tail and ran from the angry mob. People shouted out the word "coward" repeatedly, but Kevin fixated on the woman. Her dress hugged her curves, showing off her attractive toned figure. The man stepped up to the microphone, resting his hands on the edges of the podium. The woman strayed to the rear, just out of Kevin's view. He worked to force his way through the crowd, but people had stuffed themselves together trying to get close to the stage.

"I apologize, but Mr. McGilvery couldn't be here." An angry roar erupted from the crowd, drowning out the next words from the man's mouth. The man paused and patiently waited for the noise to die down before he continued. "I am Mr. Kurosawa, the chief financial officer of Labyrinth Oil." Mr. Kurosawa pointed over his shoulder towards the woman in the red dress. "And this is Miss

Eguchi, the head lawyer for our company."

Unimpressed by their titles, the crowd grew more irritated. The extreme heat wasn't helping matters. The sun's brilliant rays igniting the mob's fuse. Security guards up front struggled to keep the angry protesters from pushing their way onto the stage. Police officers called for backup, realizing that a powder keg was about to go off. Mr. Kurosawa held up his hands pleading for order.

"Pipe down!" Kevin barked. "We need to hear what he has to say." Mr. Kurosawa nodded at Kevin, but Kevin wasn't interested in Kurosawa's approval. He tried to glimpse Miss Eguchi. He hoped that his command of the crowd would impress her but he couldn't see her through the giant mob of angry fishermen.

"I am proud to announce on behalf of Labyrinth Oil we have purchased the St. John's Harbour." Mr. Kurosawa shocked the crowd. Everyone stood with their eyes wide and jaws dropped. People expected the news of an oil pump, not the acquisition of their harbour. With the crowd hushed Mr. Kurosawa foolishly carried on, not understanding what was going through the mob's mentality. "We will establish several oil pumps into the territory of the Grand Banks and the Flemish Cap."

"What's happening with the harbour?"

"How's this going to affect the fishery?"

"What are the plans for the boats docked in the harbour?"

A chorus of questions erupted from the crowd all at once. Mr. Kurosawa looked over his shoulders to Miss Eguchi, covering the microphone with his hand as they spoke.

"Where is Jonah McGilvery?"

"Get that bastard out here! I demand answers!"

"I will kill you!"

Miss Eguchi approached the dais, and they could scarcely hear her delicate voice. She had to repeat herself. "There will be no further questions."

The two Labyrinth Oil employees fled the stage, but the crowd had heard enough. Security guards and law enforcement officers pushed back as the mob tried to force their way into their path. Angry shoves and curses accompanied death threats directed towards the fleeing employees. Two guards opened the doors for them as several more security ushered them past the mob and into the building. Fishermen slammed their fists into the Plexiglas, trying to break down the door and force their way inside.

Sirens blared as the squad cars pulled into the parking lot. Cops dressed in riot gear flooded into the crowd, trying to get them to leave without further incident. Kevin backed away from the chaotic scene and got back into his truck, watching the train wreck take place from the air-conditioned cab. The riot patrols hauled away the biggest trouble makers, sending a message to the unruly mob. Police officers slammed people down onto the hot cement, placing their hands in cuffs before moving on to the next angry participant.

A vibration in Kevin's pocket drew his attention away from the rioting crowd. He reached down and pulled out his cell phone. "Hello."

"Kevin, we have a call put in on a missing person." Ali spoke softly on the other end. She was the night shift supervisor for the coast guard, which meant if she was still at work someone important had placed the call. "How long before you arrive at work?"

"I'm at the Harbour Masters now. I can be there in ten minutes." Kevin gave himself enough time to grab a coffee on the way. It was only a five-minute walk, anyway.

"I picked up your coffee on the way in." Ali's voice was heavy with sleep. "Our new boss made the call."

"I guess that's why Jonah wasn't at the conference this morning. So, who's missing?" Kevin pulled his pickup around to the edge of the parking lot, parked vehicles lined both sides of the road, but the street was empty.

"It's Mr. McGilvery. His lawyer Miss Eguchi said he took his yacht out last night and hasn't returned. They haven't been able to reach him."

Ali's statement shocked Kevin. "Have they informed the police yet?" The angry mob outside of the Harbour Masters Quarters led Kevin to believe they wouldn't find Jonah safe and sound. He knew of a few fishermen that had rap sheets longer than their resumes and regularly acted without considering the repercussions.

"The police directed her to us," Ali said sharply. "I have already been in contact with the chief of police and we are organizing the search and rescue mission."

Kevin turned down the road that lead to docks. The Canadian Coast Guard Ship *Cape Spear* was teeming with activity as workers prepared the vessel for its search and rescue mission. The white cabin sat atop the bright red hull, the lookout tower darting into the sky far above the roof. They built the CCGS *Cape Spear* for speed while still having enough room for a crew of five. Waves gently slapped the side of the forty-foot rescue ship as the calm harbour waters rose with the tide. Kevin parked his truck in his designated spot as Ali walked towards him with two white cups of coffee in her hand. Her auburn hair was unkempt and fell over her shoulders in a tangled mess, the sun giving it a radiating red aurora. Dark bags formed under her blue eyes. The effects of a long night and no sleep exaggerated the worried look on her face. "Good —"

"I don't have time for your cruel jokes today," Ali cut him off. Her grey tank top clung to her body, her skin covered in sweat from the blistering heat. "You need to get aboard now." She shoved the coffee in his face.

"I haven't even checked…"

"Everything you need is already on board and your crew is waiting for you." Ali had gained a lot of confidence since stepping into the supervisor role. She turned to leave before Kevin could say anything else. She stormed away on a mission.

Not wanting to piss her off, Kevin opened the back door of his truck to retrieve his red and white duffle bag. He slung both straps over one shoulder and walked towards his ship. His crew went about their business at a frantic pace as they loaded the last bit of cargo onto the *Cape Spear*. The dock bounced underneath his feet as Kevin walked up the ramp.

CHAPTER FOUR

Gansbaai
West Coast
South Africa

Andy Grant sat on the wharf with his legs dangling over the edge and stared down into the frothy water. The rough, chaotic ocean waters off the coast of South Africa offered Andy a strange sense of calm he couldn't explain. Three-foot waves crashed into the wood pillars that kept the wharf sturdy; all the boats bobbed up and down with the swell of the ocean. A strong breeze whipped over the water sending a spray of sea water in the air, the salty drops leaving Andy's lips dry and cracked. The film crew that funded his research were late. If they didn't arrive soon, they would have to wait for the tide to come back before they continued filming their documentary in Shark Alley.

Shark Alley was infamous for its great white sharks. The treacherous alley lay between Dyer Island and Geyser Island. Dyer Island was the home to a dwindling population of African penguins, and Geyser Island housed a colony of thousands of cape fur seals. These two islands had remained untouched by humans, both nothing more than jagged rock formations in the ocean, leaving a flourishing alley teeming with great whites in the middle. Andy had been studying the sudden reappearance of the prehistoric predators in the area. The sharks had left when a pod of orcas decimated their numbers and sent them to New Zealand. Now, after several years, they had returned to Shark Alley, bigger than ever. No one had tagged a shark in the Alley for years, and the crew had hired Andy, the former US Navy Marine diver turned cinematographer and paleobiologist, for the job.

Andy heard their truck approaching, the gravel crushed underneath its massive tires. The small fishing village of Gansbaai was impoverished and was desperate for the sharks to return. People only visited Gansbaai now when pods of whales migrated along the Western Cape coastline. The waters around the village were rich with fish, but the costs of processing and shipping their products from the isolated location proved too big a hurdle for most businesses. Few villagers owned a car, and the presence of any vehicles drew the entire village's attention. Andy glanced over his shoulders and wondered how much longer they would be.

Bright sun rays beat down on Andy's neck as he stared off at the light house at the tip of Danger Point Peninsula. A bright blue sky offered clear visibility for miles around. The waters around Birkenhead Rock, located off Danger Point, were notorious for causing over 150 ship wrecks. Even the most seasoned sailor had to be extremely cautious sailing its waters.

"Andy, you have to come see this," Derrick called

out from inside the research tent, interrupting Andy's thoughts. His research assistant was a constant pain, getting excited over every last-minute detail.

Andy stood up and headed towards the green tent, the wind whipping the flaps back and forth, the door zipper left half open. He ducked underneath and entered the temporary research lab. Derrick sat in front of his satellite laptop, the blue glow from the screen reflected off his glasses. The constant barrage of meaningless observations agitated Andy. "What is it?"

"We got a ping off the satellite tag *one five alpha*." Derrick said enthusiastically, oblivious to Andy's tone.

"We get pings off the tags all the time, Derrick. That's how we tracked the sharks from New Zealand to here." Annoyed, Andy turned to leave the tent.

"I know, but notice the region of the ping," Derrick was bursting with excitement. "It's originated from the Grand Banks of Newfoundland."

Andy stopped in his tracks. "It must be a mistake." He turned back, curious. "Who does the tag belong to?"

"It belongs to Joan of Shark," Derrick turned his laptop towards Andy. "Notice, she's been firing off signals all morning."

The bright glow of the screen was hard to look at inside the darkness of the pavilion, but the data didn't lie. Every time the shark reached the surface of the water the satellite tag would emit a signal to the receiver. Joan was active, and the receiver off the coast of Newfoundland picked up several signals over the last few hours. "Can you call the research station at the university there and make arrangements for us to get to St. John's?" Andy requested. He had first placed a tag on Joan three years ago just off the southern tip of New Zealand and followed her to Australia. They placed another tag on her there before she disappeared six months ago.

"The film crew won't be pleased with that," Derrick added.

"Well make arrangements for them too. No one ever tagged a *Carcharodon carcharias* there before." Andy had done a lot of amazing things in his career, but he had never been a pioneer. He had become an expert at tagging sharks, but he wasn't the first person. He had tracked the South African sharks to New Zealand, but wasn't the first there either. If he caught Joan of Shark in the frigid Atlantic waters off the coast off Newfoundland, maybe he wouldn't have such a hard time getting his research funded.

"What's the rush?" Derrick sat in his chair, moving sluggishly for the satellite phone. "I mean we already have a tag on her."

"The battery will die and Joan would be lost forever." A door slammed shut outside, alerting Andy to the film crews' arrival. "I'll go convince them to fund us, you make the call."

Derrick stood up, moving a little faster now as he picked up the phone. As Andy left the tent, the bright daylight forced him to squint. He instinctively held up his hand, blocking the sun from his eyes as he spotted the film crew. They had gathered in a small circle at the back of the truck as they gathered their equipment. "Hold up," Andy shouted out over the wind.

The director of the documentary turned towards

Andy. "What is it?" Ellen snapped. A sour expression on her bronzed skin, her pink lipstick smeared into the corner of her lips. She must have been in a rush; her red dress shirt was untucked and her hair was tied up in a messy bun. "We're working behind schedule."

"We should travel to Newfoundland," Andy sputtered.

"Are you kidding me?" Ellen snorted, choking back laughter. "You can't be serious."

"Joan of Shark appeared just off the coast." Andy replied, studying the disdain on Ellen's face. His response didn't impress her. The scowl grew more intense as she glared at him.

"So what? Who cares about some shark you've already tagged?" Ellen shrugged her shoulders. Andy's enthusiasm didn't affect her.

"No one has ever tagged a shark in these waters." Andy sold his proposition. "Not to mention she's a shark from right here. This changes everything we know about great whites. If we manage to catch her on film, it would be extraordinary."

"What's so important about Joan of Shark?" Ellen still wasn't buying his sale pitch. Her film crew had already unloaded their gear onto the cart and was heading down towards the boat.

"Wait up, guys." Andy held out his hand, motioning for everyone to hold on. "Ellen, Joan of Shark should just be reaching the age of maturity. I think she went to Newfoundland to mate, and if we could catch her in the act, it would be the first time anyone has ever filmed it." While no one had ever filmed a *Carcharodon carcharias* mating,

Joan of Shark didn't head into the frigid waters of the Atlantic to perform this ritual. Andy had to think of something to persuade Ellen to fund his trip, and he knew this
would catch her attention.

Ellen motioned for her crew to stop. "What makes you
think she would head into freezing cold waters to mate."

Andy had to think of something fast. "There's a reason no one has ever filmed sharks mating." Andy paused
and waited for Ellen to nod her head. "I think it's because
we've been looking in the wrong place. Get me to Newfoundland, and we can make the biggest discovery about
great whites ever. People will throw money at us to watch
this video. Research firms will pay through the nose to
be part of this groundbreaking research." Ellen stared at
Andy with a harsh expression, her pale blue eyes piercing
into his. She was studying him to see if he was bluffing.
Andy tried his best to keep a convincing look on his face.
His heart stopped beating for what seemed like an eternity as she studied him intently, watching for any sign of
deception.

"Get that gear back on the truck," Ellen ordered. "Mr.
Grant, you better be right about this, or I'll make certain
no one ever works with you again. Get your shit packed
up, and I'll make the arrangements."

"I had my assistant book the flights. I need you to pay
for them when we get to the airport." A childlike smile
crept over his steel jawline.

Ellen shook her head. "I pray for your sake that shark
is putting out." Ellen stormed off to the truck, slamming
the door behind her as she took out her phone. She rolled
the window down, a scowl on her face. "Get me some foot-

age of Shark Alley while we wait for the flight to leave. At least we will have something to show for being in this forsaken village."

Andy headed back to the tent to pack up his gear. He needed to get a tag on Joan before the battery in her tag ran out of power; he couldn't risk losing track of the creature. His whole career hung in the balance, and now he may be in over his head with Ellen. A great white shark sighting off the coast of Newfoundland was extremely rare. He didn't know why he would gamble on finding another male in the area. For the second time in his professional career he ran his mouth. The last time it had cost him his job with the Marines -- hopefully Ellen wasn't aware of what led to his dishonorable discharge from the Navy. "Derrick, get the cage ready. We need to complete a dive before we leave this place."

Gansbaai
Shark Alley
West Coast
South Africa

The waters in Shark Alley were unique. The green, murky depths gave the semblance of transparency but still veiled the ocean's deadliest predators from view. These waters were the perfect arena for them, allowing them to ambush their prey from all angles. Glimmers of silver light sparkled brightly just below the surface, the light penetrating only a few feet below the surface. Andy looked around, concealed in a foreign environment where every shadow threatened you from just beyond your reach. The speed of the demons stalking these waters made any reaction pointless. If they desired, they had the ability to stalk and ambush you without your knowledge.

Andy reached out and grasped the metal bars of his pen. No matter how many times he made the dive, he would never get accustomed to the fear that awaited him. Every passing shadow and dark crevice hid danger from view; he could never pinpoint where the threat would emerge. All he knew was the sharks in this area were attracted to the cages and had grown unafraid of them. Some sharks had grown so daring they had earned the reputation for destroying the steel enclosures, turning them into tangled, splintered fragments of metal. If he stayed down here long enough, he would eventually capture footage of a great white shark, and if he stayed down too long, he would get himself eaten. He waited for what seemed like an eternity. Something was occupying the *Carcharodon* in this area. He heard the mechanical groan as the wench raised the cage topside.

"Did you get any footage?" Derrick bellowed.

Andy shook his head. "Not this time. Do we have any old film we haven't aired yet?"

"I'll scrounge up something to fool Ellen." Derrick chuckled. "It's time to go, we will be late if we don't get a move on."

CHAPTER FIVE

CCGS **Cape Spear**
Marystown
Southern Coast of Newfoundland

The CCGS *Cape Spear* cut through the four-foot swells with efficiency as Kevin navigated his course towards Marystown, the last known position of the *Swift Current*. Equipped with an S.O.S. system, an electronic ping sounded out to the satellite every four hours. The *Cape Spear* rose on the crest of the waves and sent foamy sprays of ocean water over the bow as it plunged back down into the next wave. Kevin kept a close eye on the radar read-out, but all that popped up were small schools of fish and smaller fishing schooners. The swelling waves kept the smaller fishing dories in the harbour's shelter, but some lucky fishermen, with sturdier boats, confronted the rougher waters.

Melvin was scanning the ocean from the crow's nest with a pair of binoculars, his reflective life vest caught every glimmer of sunshine that cracked through the clouds. Dark storm clouds were slithering in from the south and a steady warm breeze had rushed in. Kevin watched as the fog rolled in over the frigid waters fed by the Labrador Current that had met the warm Pacific air. If Melvin didn't discover the boat quickly, fog would make it impossible to spot the ship. Kevin didn't like the last ping from the S.O.S system. He knew the waters around Marystown like the back of his hand from his days as a fisherman. He knew Jonah had smashed his yacht along the craggy coast.

"I can see debris hard to starboard." Melvin's voice chimed in on the walkie-talkie.

Kevin eased off the throttle and spun the ship back towards the jagged shoreline. "Copy that. How far away?"

"I'd say about half a mile," Melvin responded. "It's hard to tell with these waves."

Kevin glared out the window as Melvin climbed down the mast. Now that Kevin was heading back towards the shore, the four-foot waves rocked the boat's hull. Vibrations rattled the entire steel frame of *The Cape Spear*. Kevin had to battle with the wheel to keep his course steady. "Make sure the guys are ready," he said. "I want to find Jonah before these waves get any bigger. They built this ship for speed, not for rough seas." Kevin cursed under his breath at Ali for picking this rescue boat. He realized that time was a factor, but the waters around the Grand Banks were erratic and the impending storm surge threatened to bring in the rolling waves without warning.

"You got it, Skip." Melvin headed through the cabin and down the stairs below to round up the others.

Kevin looked down at the radar, hoping to spot any signs of the *Swift Current* nearby. Filled with green and yellow circles, the radar picked up various marine life swimming around. The screen rattled as each wave crashed into the side of the boat. Kevin pushed the throttle a little harder. He preferred to get *The Cape Spear* in a better position to break the waves.

Kevin looked through the window of the boat, pieces of broken wood and fibreglass floated in the crest of the waves. "All right," he said. "Let's bring her in and get a closer view." Kevin steered the ship towards the wreckage as it bobbed up and down with the swell of the ocean.

"Have a gander at that." Lewis leaned his hand on Kevin's shoulder, a powerful smell of caffeine and liquor on his breath.

Kevin was annoyed by the young officer. "What am I looking at Lewis?"

"The *Swift Current* has washed-up right on shore." The young search and rescue diver's voice was pompous. He yanked off his aviator sunglasses and pointed at the beached yacht. Kevin should have been looking at the rocky shore towards the *Swift Current*, but he wanted to punch Lewis in the face. His spiked black hair and thin goatee screamed hipster, but his brawny frame demanded attention. His collared shirt was unbuttoned just enough to show his shaved chest and sterling silver chain that dangled loosely from his neck. "We can anchor the boat and investigate the wreckage from the coastline."

"That's a good plan," Kevin said mockingly, not trying to hide his disdain for Lewis. "It would take hours to port if we left now. I'll throw the anchor here and you can take the lifeboat in before the tide rises and washes more debris back out into the ocean."

Lewis shook his head in disgust, taking exception to Kevin's tone. He looked like he wanted to say something before Melvin walked back inside. "Looks like we got a storm heading our way."

"Melvin take Lewis on the lifeboat with you and have a look for Mr. McGilvery." Kevin took command of his crew, the tone of his voice growing confident with power.

"Come on, lad, help me lower it into place now." Melvin took notice of the tension between the two men.

Lewis Park stood a foot taller than Kevin, with near perfect posture. The two men locked eyes, testing each other's resolve. Kevin refused to back down. "Run along with Melvin." Kevin taunted him with a sly grin.

Melvin held the door open and lingered for what seemed like an eternity before Lewis walked past Kevin, brushing by him as he strode out of the cabin. Kevin could feel his blood boiling with rage. The newest member of his crew needed to learn his rank. He was already devising a plan to teach Lewis a hard lesson about working in the ocean. He was looking back down at his sonar to gauge his depth when he noticed a large blip on the screen that disappeared just as quickly as it flashed onto the screen. Kevin tapped the filter with his knuckles, checking to see if it was malfunctioning. Outside the window, Kevin looked at Melvin and Lewis as they lowered the orange rescue craft into the rough seas then back down at the radar. He couldn't help look back down at the screen, nervously waiting for the radar to pick up the object again, but it vanished.

***

The prehistoric predator swam through the frigid current, the cold waters suppressing her appetite. She was able to sense the heartbeat of the fish with pinpoint accuracy, able to detect one from the other with ease, the hunter's abilities toned to perfection over millions of years of evolution. Its snout was covered in tiny black dots called ampullae of Lorenzini, which detected the minute electrical impulses generated by moving muscles. A passing school of fish created a sensory overload. Smaller fish gave the *Carcharodon carcharias* a wide berth, making sure they stayed far enough away that the shark's efforts weren't worth the meal. The great white had the ability to look past all the signals it received. It focused on the strange electrical impulses being sent out by the CCGS *Cape Spear*. Vibrations from the vessel created a distraction too strong to ignore, but the size of the boat kept the shark in the shadows.

Global warming's biggest concern wasn't the rising temperatures on the land. It was the deadly impact on the earth's oceans. For thousands of years the great white navigated the oceans using the magnetic fields of the earth. Now that the temperatures of the ocean were changing and the water levels were rising, those fields had evolved. These signalled the sharks to Newfoundland instead of back to South Africa. She wasn't alone on her pilgrimage. Joan sensed the other male sharks closing in on her position. She was in heat and her scent attracted several suitors, but she was avoiding them for now. All she craved was her next meal. The colder waters of the Atlantic meant she required to eat more to maintain her body temperature. As she got close enough to the boat to realize that it wasn't a whale, she lost interest. She swept her snout from side to side, probing for a meal that would be worth the expended strength. She headed back out to the deeper waters as a giant squid's beating heart grabbed her attention.

The thirty-foot *Carcharodon* raced along the rocky sea floor, her jaw left slightly ajar to allow the water to flow through her gills. Once she reached the drop-off she immediately descended into the murkier waters, getting ready to perform her assault on the giant squid. The colour of her skin allowed her to ambush her prey from below. The dark grey dermal denticles that covered her back like chain mail made her virtually invisible to prey looking down into the depths. The scales on her back resembled razor-sharp teeth. They were smooth to the touch if you ran your hand down her back, but if you went the wrong way it would shred the flesh on your hands to pieces.

Joan focused solely on the beating heart of the *Architeuthis* while still keeping track of any other signals sent her way. For now, she swam with a purpose out into the cold current around the Grand Banks towards her next meal. The powerful electrical signals from the giant squid's pulsating heart rang in Joan's head. Each heartbeat acted like a light house in the dark, lighting her way past all the other disturbances of the ocean. Sharks' survival instincts were far more sophisticated than people wanted to believe; they were not just mindless psychopaths who slaughter for sport.

The Swift Current
Marystown
Southern Coast of Newfoundland
"When is Kevin going to retire? He doesn't have a clue

about what's going on out here." Lewis Park vented his frustration to Melvin.

"I don't think that Kevin's such a bad guy." Melvin looked back at the *Swift Current*. "I'm sure he could teach you a thing or two about these waters. He's been doing this for years."

Lewis let the swell of the wave take control of the orange life raft, forcing the small vessel towards the shore. The shore line was mostly jagged rocks. The trees that managed to survive the harsh winters had their growth stunted by the strong winds. The grass was burned yellow from the relentless heat of the sun. "That don't mean much to me, Melvin," Lewis said. "Just because he's been doing something for years doesn't mean he's good at it." Lewis had developed an intense disdain for his boss since his first day on the job. "He doesn't have a clue about the science. I mean he completely ignores the effects of global warming because he doesn't believe in science." Lewis spread out his arms at his surroundings.

Melvin shook his head slowly. "There's more to this job than understanding why the ocean acts the way it does. You have to know how to handle it when you're out in her." Melvin steered the life raft into a small inlet where the waters were calmer. "Do you understand what I mean, Park?"

Lewis blushed with embarrassment. He always respected Melvin because he was good at his job and a hard worker, but he wasn't the smartest crew member in the coast guard. Lewis was more than just a little surprised to be getting solid life advice from Melvin. "Yeah, I do," Lewis mumbled. "I still don't think he should be the captain, that's all," he added.

"Maybe you're right, young fella, but it is what it is," Melvin said as he steered directly towards shore.

The wreckage of the *Swift Current* was only twenty-feet away now. Planks of wood and broken fibreglass bobbed up and down in the water all around the life boat. It had run aground during high tide, and now it was nearly ten-feet aground, left behind by the receding currents. Lewis hopped over the side of the raft. The cold waters pierced his skin like tiny icicles poking at his flesh through his rubber boots. Melvin jumped out on the other side. Both men grabbed hold of the boat and dragged it up the rocky beach until it was far enough away from the crashing waves.

"I wonder what happened?" Melvin said dumbfounded.

"Let's get closer." Lewis unzipped his jacket and tossed it in the orange life raft. The sun was beaming down on them, sweat rolled down his backside. The temperature on land was a sharp contrast to the sea. Frigid waters from the melting ice caps could be felt directly out in the water, but once you stepped foot on land the sun controlled you. As they walked towards the wreckage, the rocks slid around underneath their feet, hitting against each other. Lewis could hear the caw of seagulls over the rolling waves as they flew overhead. He looked up at the sky as the dirty white birds flew past.

Lewis approached the *Swift Current* first. Something had torn a large hole in the hull, exposing the luxurious underbelly of the yacht. "Damn, what is that stench?" Lewis caught a strong whiff of booze as he poked his head into the large gap. There were shards of glass all over the floor of the galley, Lewis spotted one cabinet door open. "Jonah left his liquor cabinet open during the crash."

"I'd say he was fetching himself a drink when it happened." Melvin helped to piece together the puzzle. "The shore is so rocky we'd never see which way he went."

Jonah McGilvery was a notorious alcoholic, and it didn't take long for Lewis to form an opinion. "I'm guessing you're right, Melvin. I'd say he came down here to fetch a drink and wasn't paying enough attention to where he was and ran his yacht right into the rocks." Lewis bent down and picked up a fragment of the rum bottle that still had the label. "Cabot Tower dark spiced rum."

"Mr. McGilvery's drink of choice." Melvin seemed to enjoy the sweet aroma of the liquor.

"I take it it's yours too." Lewis smirked. Melvin bent down to pick up a piece of broken glass, rubbing his finger over the sticky surface. He put his finger in his mouth once he had enough of the substance on it to taste. "Well what's the final consensus?" Lewis asked.

"Tastes like salt water and spiced rum," Melvin said with a sour expression on his face. "Not the way my woman mixes my drinks."

"To each their own I suppose," Lewis joked. "Can you get on the radio and let Kevin know we will probably find Mr. McGilvery in one of the bar's in Marystown."

"You think he ran off towards town?" Melvin questioned.

"Let's hope so. If not, the poor man got himself lost in the woods over there. I guess we will need to alert search and rescue just in case, but I'm guessing even if Jonah was loaded drunk, he would still see the lights." Lewis stepped inside the *Swift Current*, the glass crunching underneath his boots. Looking around the galley, Lewis searched for any signs of what happened to Jonah. The wooden bar had a small red stain that had dripped down over the side of the bar. Lewis walked over to get a better view and it became glaringly obvious that it was a blood stain. A tiny piece of blood-stained tooth had fallen into the sink. The sudden impact must have caused Jonah to smash his face into the bar as he was taking a drink. He looked down into the garbage can but there weren't any bloody rags or tissue inside. Whatever happened must have caused Jonah to run topside in a hurry. Flecks of blood led towards the ladder up to the deck. The bright red drops stained the shiny metal surface all the way up. Lewis headed back outside, not wanting to disturb the blood stains on the ladder in case the police needed to investigate.

Melvin was sitting on the edge of the orange life raft with the radio in his hand. The sun glistened off the white caps behind him, making his figure nothing more than a silhouette against the bright blue backdrop. The CCGS *Cape Spear* cut through the waves out in the rough seas as it headed towards the port of Marystown. Lewis walked around the yacht and searched for any more signs of blood against the rock in a vain effort. If Mr. McGilvery had abandoned ship, the waves would have washed any evidence away. The *Cape Spear* was tilted towards the water at a slight angle on its port side. Lewis could see the railing had been bent outwards, which caught his attention; every other sign of damage pointed to a crash except that one section of railing. He figured that it must have been from an earlier accident that had never been repaired in ages, but Lewis still got closer for a better look.

Something was lodged in the wood just below the rail. Lewis reached up and felt something jagged embedded in the decking. He was able to get just enough of a grip on it to dislodge it. He pulled down the object and held it in his hand. The sunlight glared off the surface of the giant two-inch tooth in the palm of his hand. The serrated tip came to a deadly point, and the edge of the tooth was razor-sharp along the outside. "What the hell?" Lewis said aloud. He tucked the tooth into his pocket for safekeeping. He needed to call his ex-girlfriend at the Marine Institute to identify which species of fish had left this massive tooth behind. Lewis looked back out towards the vast ocean as a chill ran down his spine at the thought of heading back out there in that tiny life raft. "Fuck me."

CHAPTER SIX

The Marine Institute
St. John's, NL

Kate Hamilton sat in front of her high-powered microscope looking at a slide of bacteria found in a codfish. A restaurant had claimed a local fisherman had sold them a batch of tainted fish caught off the shores of Cape Race. Her students had prepared the sample under her supervision during class earlier, but now she sat in the laboratory by herself. Her desk overlooked two rows of five workstations that ran down the middle of the classroom. Each workstation had its own wash sink, black countertops, and stainless-steel cabinets underneath. Two long countertops lined the walls that ran the entire length of the room. They had built shelves above and below the counters to store the various equipment needed to run the labs.

The room was eerily quiet, the students all gone to lunch in the cafeteria at the other side of campus. Kate didn't like being a teacher, but it was part of her duties at the Marine Institute. They agreed to fund her research on the cod fishery, and she only needed to teach two classes, but she didn't like being in front of so many people and having to speak. She looked down at the watch on her slender wrist and could feel her stomach tighten: only another twenty minutes until her next class. Once her final class of the day finished, she would be free of teaching for the weekend and left alone to work in her lab. While many considered Kate to be beautiful, she didn't have time for dating. She was happiest when she could immerse herself in her work; she knew what she was doing would change the way people viewed the oceans. Kate did her thesis on the effects of the rising sea levels caused by the effects of global warming and its effect on the marine ecosystem. Her study had earned her recognition from the entire scientific community, and the grant at the Marine Institute here in St. John's. Kate theorized that the health of the Grand Banks off the southern coasts of Newfoundland was vital not only to the island's economy, but it was also a key indicator of the effects of global warming. As the polar ice caps melted into the Arctic oceans, the frigid water poured into the strong Labrador Current. This cold layer of water was changing the ocean's ecosystem, and there wasn't a better place on earth for studying the effects than right here. Species of fish only found in the Arctic Ocean drifted south towards the densely populated fishing grounds of the Grand Banks. Fisherman reported catching several new species in their cod fishing nets. Reports of Greenland sharks escalated to a daily occurrence. Whale migration patterns changed, bringing more whales down the Labrador Current than ever before.

Kate heard the murmur of students as they flooded back into the halls. Students started getting ready for their next class, opening their lockers and chatting about what their plans for the weekend. There was a time when she used to be just like them, but that seemed like such a long time ago even though she had only graduated three years before. Kate looked back down into the microscope. It was just another sample of tissue from a healthy cod. The owner of the restaurant didn't accept that they hired a shitty cook. She placed another slide underneath the microscope to confirm what the other twenty slides had already told her. The door creaked open. Kate didn't want to make small talk with any of her students right now.

"Hello, Kate." A familiar voice from her past sent her heart racing.

Kate looked over at her old boyfriend Lewis Park, standing in the door frame. "Hey, Lewis." Kate's voice squeaked like a teenager. Lewis was leaning against the frame, biting onto an arm of his aviator glasses, his features scrunched up nervously on his face. "I'm surprised to see you."

"You look good." Lewis stared down at the floor immediately after the words left his mouth, his cheeks turning red. "Long time no see."

Kate wanted to rush over to him, unable to decide if she wanted to hit him or hug him. "You never called." She wished she hadn't said that, but her anger muddled her thoughts. "I didn't think you wanted to stay in Newfoundland?"

Lewis fidgeted with his glasses. "Listen, I'm not here to talk about that."

"Then what are you doing here?" Kate cut him off. She had felt betrayed when he moved away, but it had devastated her when she discovered he moved back home without telling her.

"I need your help with a work-related problem." Lewis tried to change the topic, his deep blue eyes avoiding eye contact with her. "Would you examine something I found?"

The hallway grew louder with noise now as her students made their way back to their classes. Kate just wanted five minutes with him. She wanted to get an apology or at least an explanation. "Can you come back after class?" Kate offered in hopes he would agree.

Lewis walked over to her desk and took out a clear plastic bag with a tooth in it. "I'll come back later." Lewis placed the bag down on her desk. "When would be a good time?"

Kate looked down at the razor-sharp looking tooth and recognized it. "It belongs to *Architeuthis dux*." Kate picked the bag up and handed it back to Lewis, who had a confused expression on his face. "A giant squid common to the waters around Newfoundland."

"A giant squid left this tooth behind?" Lewis looked like he had seen a ghost, his skin turned a pasty white.

"Razor-sharp teeth line their beaks in rows." Students filed into the classroom. "My lab will be over in three hours if you need any further explanation."

Lewis tucked the bag back into his pocket. "Listen, I'll drop by sometime if you'd like, but I need to get back to work."

Kate wanted him to come back, but she refused to seem desperate. She sat at her desk in silence, glancing at her students as they settled away behind their stations. The room filled with the sound of zippers opening and closing, books hitting the desks, and chit-chat between the students. "Mr. Park, if you need to see me, I will be here in my laboratory during the hours posted on my door. Now if you will excuse me, I have a class to teach."

Lewis sauntered out of the room, pausing briefly at the door to study her timetable. He looked back at her as he put his sunglasses back on, an awkward smile on his face. "I'll talk to you later." Lewis stood head and shoulders above everyone as he joined the crowd. Kate's face flushed with embarrassment. She prayed that her students didn't notice. "All right, class, open your books to chapter seven. We will learn about the different diseases that affect our fish in the Atlantic Ocean."

CHAPTER SEVEN

Outer Cove
Logy Bay
Newfoundland

David stood on the edge of the bank, staring down at the rocky beach of Outer Cove wondering if he could drive his truck down to the beach. He didn't want to lug his kayak down the steep path, but he saw no alternative way down. His eyes moved back and forth from the rock pools that spread out across the shoreline and the breaking waves as they crashed against the rocks. He felt the rejuvenating energy of the sun against his backside warming his body. Seagulls sang their high-pitched notes from their perches along the jagged coast.

"Well, what's the verdict?" David's wife, Alice, called from the passenger seat. The natural cadence of of the sea mesmerized David, the salty smell of the water and the soft twinkling of sunlight glistening off the waves capturing his attention. "Earth to David."

"Park the pickup and we will have to carry the kayak's down," David answered without twisting around. The couple had heard about a pod of killer whales in Logy Bay and wanted to get a closer look for themselves, but found all the whale sight-seeing tours booked solid. They had used to kayak before the kids were born and didn't think it would too troublesome to take up again.

David returned his focus towards shore and observed the rushing waves as they collided with the jagged outcrops, sending sprays of ocean water high into the sky. Littered with pebbles, burnt logs and discarded campfires, the small beachhead below was a popular destination amongst the locals. The calm waters below were enough to launch their kayaks and give them time to get used to the swell of the waves. Whispers of the ocean breeze tousled David's long blond mane. He closed his eyes and took a deep breath of the poignant salty air.

"David, are you going to help me, or should I carry both myself." Alice had grown impatient, their daughter fraying her last nerve the night before.

"Coming, honey." David hopped over the tiny white fence. The chipped paint and splintered wood reflected years of neglect. "Sorry, why don't you head down to the beach and relax. I'll bring them down."

Alice stood with her hands on her hips, her blue and green wetsuit clinging to her slender frame. She tied her auburn hair into a messy bun atop her head. Her freckles seemed to multiply with the exposure to the sunlight. Her emerald eyes glimmered with the sparkle from the ocean. "Are you sure?" Her voice softened.

"Yeah, I'm sure, honey. We have lots of time." David followed his wife's butt as she strolled away with a sly smile on his face. "Not so fast."

Alice peeked over her shoulder; a playful grin painted

on her lips. "You're sweet today." She giggled. "What do you crave?"

David winked at his wife, the intoxicating aurora of the sea lifting away his cares. "I see no one around."

"In your dreams, David." Alice walked down the bank and stopped just before she disappeared from view. "Isn't the ocean just dreamy."

David left the kayaks in the bed of the truck and ran down the bank after his partner.

Logy Bay
Newfoundland

David could feel his shoulders growing sore as he paddled through the growing swells protecting the cove. His kayak would ride up the crest of a wave and plummet down into the next, sending sprays of salty mist into his face. The strong breeze made the ocean choppy. He kept looking over his shoulders to make sure Alice was close by. She showed no signs of fatigue, keeping up with him as they headed towards the eighteen-foot whale watching boat. The owner painted the boat a sleek black with a deep red stripe along the top. Silver rails lined the back of the ship. A group of excited whale watchers had gathered on the far side, huddled against the rail. They were all taking pictures and pointing out to sea. It had to be the pod of killer whales.

"We're almost there." David tried to hide his fatigue, but he found it difficult to control his heavy breathing.

"You going to make it?" Alice said sarcastically. "I thought you'd have more energy after what I did for you."

"I would do that all day, but don't worry about me. I'll race you there," David called out playfully.

"Of course, you would do that all day, you did nothing." Alice paddled faster, gaining on David.

David churned his arms faster, the muscles in his shoulders growing tighter with every stroke. The kayak cut through the waves, icy cold water washing over David's lap. His neck muscles tightened. He lowered his head and forced his arms to keep moving. His lungs burned now and he couldn't catch his breath. Alice called out his name from behind. At least he wouldn't lose this race.

"Look up, David!" Alice screamed; her voice full of shrill panic.

David opened his eyes and saw nothing but the black wall of the schooner just feet in front of him. He wouldn't have time to turn out of the way now. His only chance of avoiding a collision was to stop. Without thinking, David drove the paddles into the water to slow his kayak. His boat turned sideways just as a wave crashed into the side, tipping it over. Trapped for what seemed like an eternity, David found himself upside down in the ice-cold water. He swallowed a mouthful of the salty brine. The frigid cold waters stung his skin all over. David opened his eyes, the salt burning into them. He tried to orient himself so he could roll the kayak back over, but he couldn't gather enough momentum to swing it right side up. A powerful blow struck his arm and David screamed out in pain. Bubbles of air escaped his mouth and floated up to the surface. His stomach twisted into tight knots as his mind raced with the possibilities of what had struck him. He twisted his neck to see a paddle thrust into the water. David reached out and grasped hold of the wooden shaft, and, before he knew it, he saw the burning yellow sun as he breached the surface. Gasping for air, David looked over at Alice. "I'm okay."

"You sure?" Alice asked, concerned. "You seem like you swallowed a lot of water."

Ocean water filled David's mouth with a bitter taste, his lungs burning from oxygen deprivation. "At least I won the race," David tried to joke as he spit up water. His whole body was shaking from the cold.

"I should have left you down there." Alice rolled her eyes at him.

"Everything all right down there?" The captain of the ship called out from behind a giant wooden steering wheel.

"Yes, everyone is okay, thanks for helping." Alice answered.

"Come around this side of the boat. The orcas are putting on a show for us." The captain pointed out towards the deep blue sea.

"Are you up for this?" Alice turned her kayak to face David. "We don't have to do this if you don't want to."

"We came all this way. It would be a shame to miss it." David mustered all of his remaining strength and paddled his way around the ship, Alice keeping right behind his slow pace.

As they rounded the nose of the ship, they saw three orcas breaching the water playfully, the water dripping from their slick black and white bodies, their giant black dorsal fins standing five-feet tall. They were playing with something, bouncing it high in the air amongst each other.

They seemed to be putting on a show for the whale watchers. David's kayak rocked up and down from the rippled waves as the killer whales' bodies slammed back down into the ocean. The two larger males were over twenty-feet long and weighed over five tonnes, while the smaller female was about eighteen feet and four tonnes. They were playing with their food, a seven-foot shark with a pure white belly and grey back.

"Is that a baby great white shark?" Alice asked in astonishment.

"It can't be. I don't think I've ever heard of a white shark in these waters." David had grown up on the seas and never encountered a great white shark before. "It's a porbeagle." Killer whales were edging closer to them without either of them noticing before it was too late. The large male orca flung the dead fish high in the air straight towards David. A thousand-pound carcass crashed into his kayak, splintering the plastic and sending a flood of ice-cold water over him. "Jesus Christ!" David screamed, a wave of panic washing over him. "Get me the fuck out of here!" He abandoned the sinking kayak and swam towards the boat, looking over his shoulders as the orcas kept creeping closer to retrieve their prey.

The captain of the boat threw David a life preserver and pulled him in as soon as he got in it. Alice paddled her canoe quickly. Someone threw her a line to pull her up once she was close enough. Alice ran over and wrapped David in a bear hug once they were both on board. "It's not my day is it?" David groaned; his entire body ached.

Alice laughed. "It definitely isn't your day, sweetheart."

The crew of the boat threw a fishing net down to catch the shark, the green threads wrapped over the lifeless body as the net sank into the ocean. It took all four of the crew plus four more of the passengers to drag the corpse onto the deck.

Something had torn the shark's stomach open with extreme precision. The insides of the dead creature were still intact. Its wet black eyes looked off into the distance. Rows of razor-sharp teeth lined its jaws in a viscous looking smile. The shark had no visible scars aside from the clean cut that ran the length of the pristine white stomach. "Well, I'll be surprised if that isn't a great white shark." The captain stood at the pectoral fin of the lifeless shark. "It looks like a juvenile too," he said to one of his crew.

CHAPTER EIGHT

Marystown
The Fisherman's Landing

Cigarette smoke veiled the air of the primitive bar. The patrons of The Fisherman's Landing stood just outside on the deck overlooking the harbour. Kevin walked over to the bar and grabbed a stool. The bartender sauntered over; a dish rag slung over her shoulder. "What can I get for you?" A woman in her thirties, wearing a pink and blue plaid shirt covered in liquor stains leaned in to find out what Kevin demanded.

"I'm just here searching for a friend. Have you noticed him here?" Kevin brought up a picture of Jonah McGilvery on his phone that he'd found on the local news website.

The waitress reached into her slacks pocket and pulled out a pair of red-rimmed reading glasses. She had a look at the picture and shook her head. "Can't say I did, sweetheart." Her voice was dry and raspy. She drew up a glass of water and took a deep drink to clear her throat. "Is that the fellow on the news that people are saying went missing last night out on the water?"

Kevin nodded his head in agreement. "The same guy,

honey." An intoxicated man bumped into Kevin's arm, spilling his white Russian all over Kevin's pants. "Excuse me," Kevin said, raising his arms in the air, revealing his displeasure with the man's clumsiness. The man didn't even seem to notice he wasn't alone at the bar. He stumbled his way towards the washroom, his trousers already unzipped.

"Could you excuse me a second. I need to call Gary's wife to come get him." The waitress excused herself to make the phone call.

Kevin walked through the dank bar, the floor boards creaking beneath his feet as he made his way towards the balcony door. The owners filled the room with round tables chest high; the dark oak wood hadn't aged well. The bar stools had no backs. Anyone that had stayed inside leaned into the table, slouching with their drink grasped desperately in their fist. With the fishing grounds around the Grand Banks closed, it sent the ability of the men to earn a living and their emotional status plummeting to depressing levels. Kevin was glad he had changed out of his work clothes before coming to The Fisherman's Landing. He would have been asking for a confrontation wearing his uniform here.

Pushing the door open, the sea air and smoke mixed into a comforting scent. Kevin closed his eyes, drawing in a deep breath. The sunlight glared off the water in the harbour, virtually blinding him as he opened his eyes. Angry fishermen filled the patio with angry conversations and despair for the future. No one paid him any attention, their faces buried in their drinks. Kevin pulled out a pack of smokes and stuck a fag in his mouth. "Can I borrow a light?" Kevin said as the cigarette dangled from his lips. A man flicked a yellow lighter and held it for Kevin, a tiny orange flicker lighting his cigarette as he puffed on the filter. "Thanks."

The tired-looking man stared at Kevin with bloodshot eyes. Dry ocean air chaffed his lips and his nose red from sunburn. "No problem, stranger. What brings you all the way down here?"

Kevin pulled up the picture of Jonah and showed it to the fisherman. "Have you seen this man around here?"

A scowl caused deep creases to appear in the man's thickened skin. "It's a good thing I didn't because I'd give that bastard a piece of my mind."

"What's going on, Al?" one of the other men inquired.

"This fucker is down here seeking for the man responsible for the closure of the fishery." Spittle flew from Al's mouth as his face turned rosy red, the veins in his neck popping out with the surge in blood pressure.

"They reported him missing last night, his yacht washed up just outside town." Kevin struggled to explain himself. Deep down he hated Jonah McGilvery just as much as they did. "I'm just trying to do my job, folks." Angry eyes glared at Kevin; the mob of unemployed fisherman began to surround him. "I don't agree with what he did either." Kevin glanced over his shoulder; an immense man cut off the doorway. His chest muscles bulged out of open plaid shirt, his forearms thick with muscles and swelling veins.

"I'd say you're searching in the wrong place for that son of a bitch." Al drove his index finger into Kevin's rib cage, driving him back with a slight jolt.

"Ease up, pal, I'm not looking for trouble." Kevin frantically searched for a way off the deck, but the drop was too far and the landing full of jagged rocks. The only way out was through the door and he didn't stand a chance against the behemoth blocking the way.

"I'd say Mr. McGilvery is a bloated corpse out there somewhere." Al pointed out towards the harbour. "Hopefully they never find his body."

"I couldn't agree with you more," Kevin stammered desperately trying to smooth over the situation.

"This is your only opportunity to leave." Al's breath was heavy with the smell of booze and stale stench of smoke. The gargantuan man held the door open for Kevin. "Anyone who's with Labyrinth Oil isn't welcome around here. Go on back to town and make sure that you spread the message around."

"I certainly will." Kevin left The Fisherman's Landing as quickly as his legs would carry him without looking back. He nearly tripped up in the uneven dirt parking lot. The sound of gravel crunching behind him, he threw open the door and jumped into his truck without waiting to see who was approaching. Kevin tried to grab his keys out of his pocket, but his jeans were too tight. A sharp knock on the window forced Kevin to look up.

"Don't mind that old fool. He's just had too much to drink and not enough to eat." The bartender had followed him out of the bar. The bright sunlight gave her dark hair a deep red glow.

Kevin allowed himself to relax enough to catch his breath. He stretched his leg out and forced his fingers far enough into his pants to grasp his keys. He turned on his truck and rolled down the window. "Does he always threaten people like that?"

"There's something you need to understand, young feller." She leaned against the door of the truck, resting her forearm on the window sill. "That man you're looking for stole something from these men that you can't replace."

"What's that?" Kevin asked foolishly.

"Their livelihood," the bartender said with a snarl. "That man got what he had coming to him if you ask me. Maybe it would be best if you left well enough alone if you catch my drift."

Kevin nodded in agreement. "I do." He put the truck into gear and eased out of the parking lot. Once his tires hit the paved main road, he pushed down on the gas. He looked in his rear-view mirror. The woman was still watching him as he drove out of sight. Kevin didn't know what happened to Jonah, but he was sure that they would not find his body. He knew he should tell the police about what had happened at The Fisherman's Landing, but his hands shook in fear of retaliation. He didn't want to join Jonah McGilvery as an ornament at the bed of the briny deep.

North Atlantic Ocean

The *Carcharodon* swam through the second largest ocean in the world, its waters covering twenty percent of the earth's surface. Bounded on the west by North and South America, this massive body of water was home to a vast array of wildlife. Frigid waters from the melting ice caps in the Arctic Ocean fed into the North Atlantic Ocean. These cold waters led the migrating packs of humpback whales further south to the shores of Newfoundland. The flutter of a whale's heartbeat alerted the apex predator to a source of food. Its muscles sending off signals as it beat its tail fin against the surface of the ocean. She continued to follow the continental shelf, keeping well below the surface of the water and staying hidden from view.

Nature built the great white for speed. Her triangle shaped snout allowed her to cut through the waters with ease. A thousand electrical impulses signalled from the sea floor, but her brain tuned them all out, her focus remaining on the whale's heartbeat. She cruised along the steep drop off, her body more accustomed the pressures of the deeper waters. Her stomach didn't demand as much nourishment down below. Rays of light from the yellow sun high in the sky ignited her appetite, but they failed to reach her down here. Able to turn her brain into cruise control, the shark could limit her energy depletion as she swam six-hundred metres below the surface, her mouth open in a sinister smile as she followed the electrical beacon towards the humpback whale.

CCGS **Cape Spear**
Marystown
Atlantic Ocean

"So, you're trying to tell me a squid killed Jonah?" Kevin couldn't accept what Lewis was telling him. "I thought you were supposed to be the smart one."

Lewis clasped the tooth in his fist. "I think it's an option we have to look at."

"I'm listening. I'm just having a hard time trying to figure out if you're trying to pull my leg or not." Kevin stared into Lewis's eyes but couldn't detect anything but the young man's concerned glare. "Tell me again where you found it?"

"I discovered it lodged it into the decking of the hull, right below the rail." Lewis held up the tooth between his thumb and index finger. "It broke from the creature's jaw." The light glistened off the razor-sharp tooth, the edges jagged and razor sharp.

Kevin didn't want to go to the police and propose a giant squid had ingested Mr. McGilvery. He was sure they'd laugh him out of the station. "Listen, Lewis, I recognize we don't get along but don't think I'm dismissing your opinion because I don't like you. I can't ever remember hearing about a squid that ate someone. It sounds fake." Kevin felt the swell of the ocean grow stronger as they left the safety of Marystown. "Just listen to what you're suggesting."

"I agree it makes little sense, but what else do you think happened?" Lewis raised his voice at Kevin, becoming frustrated that he wasn't listening to him.

"If you'd have been at The Fisherman's Landing with me, I know you'd come to the same conclusion as me." Kevin pushed the throttle forward. The engines rumbled below sending a wave of vibrations through the deck. "I suspect one of those fishermen may have seen his yacht last night and got rid of him."

"Are you kidding me? You're telling me somebody sailed out to the *Swift Current*, climbed aboard the yacht and killed Jonah." Lewis slammed the tooth down on the control panel. "And planted a fucking giant squid's tooth to cover their tracks."

"Listen, kid, you're not the one who has to get in front of the cops and tell them what happened. For now, we will file a missing person's report." Kevin reached out and snatched the tooth. "I'll mention we found this on board the *Swift Current*. But I ain't going to be the one to propose a fucking squid ate Jonah McGilvery!" Kevin yelled at his subordinate.

"Is everything okay in here?" Melvin asked, materializing out of thin air.

"Everything is splendid," Lewis muttered as he trudged away.

"What's the issue with you fellows this time?" Melvin stuck his nose where it didn't belong, trying to be the negotiator between the two again.

"We don't agree on something, that's all you need to know." Kevin was agitated.

"You don't say. Wish I had a nickel for every time that happened. I wouldn't have to work on this ship and listen to you two bicker at each other." Melvin didn't seem like he would leave soon, plunking himself down in the captain's chair.

"Why don't you make yourself at home, Melvin?" Melvin annoyed Kevin, but he hid it in behind a sarcastic tone.

"Saw no one else sitting in it." Melvin eyed the controls. "Ain't nobody watching the speed. We in a rush to get back?"

"Maybe we are, Melvin." Kevin leaned his head back to crack his neck, trying anything possible to mitigate the stress he was suffering.

"We are pushing the ship awfully hard, might burn out the engine in these rough waves." Melvin didn't wait for permission before easing off the throttle. "You're pissed off, but you still have to keep control of things around here."

"You're not questioning my decision-making skills, are you?" The accusation insulted Kevin.

"All I'm saying is everything is in the red and that ain't safe. You can take it whatever way you want to." Melvin met Kevin's glare with resolve, not backing down from his boss.

"You think Lewis should be in charge, don't you?" Kevin's blood was boiling, jealousy creeping over him.

"I expect he could handle this ship." Melvin paused. "I recognize you can when you got your head on straight. You won't be on the CCGS *Cape Spear* much longer, and this may be my last time coming out here. I've seen enough of the ocean to last me ten lifetimes. I've seen the sea destroy people's lives in all kinds of ways. I'm getting out of her way before my luck runs out. You can't beat her but many men have joined her."

"Melvin, what's your point?" Kevin had heard Melvin say he was quitting before, and he was expecting it. Every time they couldn't find a body or something bad happened, Melvin would always have second thoughts about his job.

"My point is we need to train people like Lewis. As long as people work in the ocean, people will get lost in it. They'll need rescuing. I'm on your side here. Lewis has a lot to learn, but, given the chance, he could do this job better than either one of us."

"Melvin, would you mind watching after things up here? I need to go take a break. I need to gather my thoughts." Kevin looked at Melvin who nodded his head in silence.

Kevin headed down below to the break room to find Lewis sitting at the table, playing with a deck of cards. When Lewis realized it was Kevin standing there, he went back to playing his game of solitaire without saying another word. Kevin walked over to the fridge and pulled open the door. The shelves were bare except for some bottles of water and packages of pepperoni and cheese. He grabbed a snack and sat directly across from Lewis.

"You have something you want to say?" Lewis didn't look up from his card game.

"I need something from you." Kevin waited until Lewis met his gaze. "I need you to investigate into this further." He placed the tooth on the table.

Lewis reached out and swiped the tooth off the table before Kevin changed his mind. "Why? Will the cops will be interested in it?"

Kevin still didn't feel comfortable going to the cops with this information, but he remembered they weren't the ones who issued the search and rescue mission. "People working at Labyrinth Oil will need to determine if they're putting their workers in danger. They have over fifty people getting ready to head down to the sea floor working on that oil line."

"You will still let the cops know about all of this right?" Lewis lowered his voice.

"Don't worry about it. You can do it yourself. I'm letting you take the lead on this, kid." Kevin tore open the plastic wrapper, a flood of relief washing over him.

"Are you kidding me?" Lewis was dumbfounded.

"I kid you not." Kevin tore a piece of pepperoni off with his back teeth. "I'll even help you every step of the way. It's long past overdue you start taking some responsibility around here."

"Uh... thanks, Kevin. I really appreciate this, and I won't let you down." Lewis held out his hand.

Kevin reached out and shook Lewis's hand, both men squeezing as hard as possible to prove their dominance. "You won't, Lewis." Kevin was glad to be free of this case. As soon as the news caught wind of the suspicious nature of Jonah McGilvery's disappearance the allegations would promptly follow. The police would start questioning some local fisherman, and Kevin was glad that he wasn't going to be linked with case.

Canadian Coast Guard
Dock
St. John's Harbour

Kevin sat alone in his office. A soft blue paint coated the walls. The lone window in the room faced the harbour, his view of the dark blue waters obstructed by the ships anchored just outside. On his glass desk rested a mountain of paperwork held in place by a whale-shaped paperweight. An air conditioner was blasting cold air at him from the corner as it swiveled back and forth. Kevin covered the wall with an oversized map of the waters around Newfoundland and the Eastern Coast of Labrador. The light in the ceiling was dim. The bulb flickered as the filament neared the end of its life.

Kevin had easily tricked Lewis into taking the bait. Now that the kid was going to be running the show and have his face in the media, Kevin was apprehensive of retribution from the fisherman in Marystown. He knew the best thing to do was to call in an anonymous tip, letting Lewis handle the media when they wanted an interview. This was almost too perfect. Lewis was so eager for control that Kevin didn't even have to convince him. He opened the bottom drawer of his desk and pulled out a silver flask. He unscrewed the cap letting out the oak-aged fragrance of whisky. Kevin gasped as the warm liquid took his breath away. The amber liquid burned the whole way down. The first swig of alcohol was always the hardest, but with every mouthful it got easier. He took another swig of the bittersweet drink, this time allowing the taste to linger on his tongue a little longer.

Picking up the phone, Kevin dialed the number to the police station. "St. John's Police Department, how may I direct your call?" a tired voice asked.

"I'd like to speak to the agent handling the McGilvery case." Kevin lowered the tone of his voice, trying to mimic an elderly gentleman.

"Just one moment please."

Kevin listened to the background music as he waited for his call to be transferred through to the detective handling the case. Kevin took another sip of the whisky and determined that he had built up enough liquid courage to follow through with the hoax. He felt his body temperature rising as the alcohol filled his empty stomach. He waited impatiently, thumbing through some paperwork he had left on his desk. His lips curled into a frown as he stared at the insurance papers requiring his signature. It still turned his stomach why he needed it. People had tried to sue the Canadian Coast Guard when they couldn't rescue their boats even though they had saved their lives. People could be so ungrateful.

"Hi, this is Detective Bowers. You possess information regarding the McGilvery case?" The young man's voice startled Kevin, bringing him back to the phone call.

"Yes, I have reason to believe a fisherman may have killed Mr. McGilvery." Kevin struggled to make his voice sound hoarse in an effort to camouflage his true voice.

"Now why would you suggest that, sir?" Detective Bowers sounded incredulous.

"Well, I overhead a guy from the Canadian Coast Guard talking to one of his employees about what he found below deck of the *Swift Current*," Kevin lied.

There was an abrupt silence. "Did you happen to catch the Coast Guard's name?"

"It was Lewis I think." Kevin made it sound like he was trying to recall. "Lewis Park."

CHAPTER NINE

20,000 ft above sea level
South Atlantic Ocean
Flight 148CC

Andy Grant looked out the tiny porthole window of
the plane. The clouds parted just enough for him to see the
glistening waters of the Atlantic Ocean far below. The cabin of the plane was darkened, the lights turned off for the
lengthy journey from South Africa to New York. A scattered dull yellow glow from the overhead light dimly lit
the cabin. Most of the other passengers on the flight were
getting some shut-eye, sleep escaped Andy; he was too
nervous. If they would lost track of Joan and this whole
trip would be a failure. Derrick sat in the seat across the
aisle from him, his head titled back and his jaw hanging
open, drool sliding down his chin from the corner of his
mouth.

Andy reached up and turned his light back on to study
his notes on the migration patterns of the *Carcharodon carcharias*, working to slice the theory together. The words
were barely visible from the dim glow. Luckily, Andy had
them memorized, but he liked the visual keys that jogged

his memory. Some scientists observed that sharks used not only their ampullae of Lorenzini to track prey, they also used their amplified sensory receptors to follow the earth's magnetic fields from place to place. The powerful force fields generated deep below the earth's crust kept them on track when crossing the vast oceans. Knowing this would help explain how Joan of Shark found her way back to her species' pupping ground. He needed to back up his theory with scientific data in case he was wrong about the reason Joan made her way to Newfoundland. Ellen would try to end his career otherwise.

He looked over to where she was sitting, her lustrous black hair drawn up in a compact bun and her perfectly pressed pant suit screaming professionalism. She was fingering the pages of a pamphlet, her head slanted down reading an article intently. Deep shadows cast across her face from the light above, smoothing out her harsh features.

A steward bearing a black vest over a white dress shirt pushed a grey trolley down the aisle, not bothering to wake the sleeping passengers. He paused next to Ellen, leaning in to ask her if she wanted anything in a hushed voice. She leaned in; her bright pink lipstick close to the nape of his neck as she whispered back to him. Andy felt a sudden twinge of jealousy wash over him, his blood pressure rising. At first, he didn't enjoy working with Ellen, but she gradually grew on him over months of working, her beauty hidden behind an almost permanent scowl and disdain for struggling to make it in a male dominated industry. The steward poured a glass of water and handed her a small pack of cookies. He leaned back in; his lips close to her ears as he whispered something to her that made her giggle. Her face blushed underneath her tanned complexion, her pale blue eyes looked vibrant as they locked eyes. The steward handed Ellen a piece of paper and a pen. She scribbled something on it and handed it to him. He tucked it in his chest pocket, patting his chest to confirm it was in there before making his way to Andy.

"Good day, sir." The South African man leaned in close, his tone low but firm. "What can I get for you?"

Andy shook his head. "Nothing for me, thanks." Andy looked at his name tag. "Appreciate the offer, Will."

"Really? I'm sure I must have something that will interest you," Will said with a smile as he tugged open a tiny drawer.

Even though Andy had never showed any interest in Ellen before, he found himself jealous and resentful at the man. Will's black hair was styled into a tight fade, an impeccably groomed goatee on his chin. "I'm sure, pal," Andy said a little too loudly. Ellen turned her head towards them.

"I have coffee, everyone loves coffee." Will held up a silver pot and white Styrofoam cup.

Andy just wanted him gone, so he figured it be quicker if he agreed. "Fresh milk and one sugar."

"I knew it. I always aim to please my passengers." He poured the coffee into the cup, slowly adding the milk and sugar. The bitter scent of coffee filled the air, swirls of steam rising from the piping hot liquid. "Here you are, sir."

"Thanks," Andy said, the warmth from the coffee wafted over his face as he raised the cup to his lips. He blew on it, sending ripples over the surface.

"One last thing, sir." Will reached into his breast pocket and took out the folded piece of paper, handing it over to Andy.

Andy opened the paper and laughed. "Get some rest, you have a long day ahead tomorrow," he read the note out loud. "Thank you, Will." Andy wanted to deliver a note back, but he wasn't certain if Ellen was flirty or serious.

"Enjoy the rest of your flight, sir." Will pushed the trolley further down the aisle and out of view.

Andy looked back towards Ellen, and, much to his chagrin, she had her nose buried back in the magazine. He thought he could see a grin curve up on the corner of her face. Andy reached up, turning off the overhead light. He thought about going to sleep, but the steaming hot liquid in his hand suggested otherwise. Andy took a sip of the coffee and scrunched up his face. It tasted like dirt sifted through a sock, the vile drink sitting in his hands futilely. He didn't want to drink it, but the thought of spilling the steaming hot water over his lap was adequate to keep him alert. "God damn it, Will," Andy muttered under his breath, as he looked down at the coffee grinds floating in his mug.

"Since we both can't sleep, do you mind running me through why we left shark alley to find a shark in some place I've never heard off." Ellen startled Andy; he hadn't noticed her approach. He shifted over to the empty seat next to the window. He looked out the window to avoid showing too much interest in her presence, but his heart was beating a little faster now.

"Joan has reached the age where she will search for a mate." Andy had been tracking this shark for years now and was confident she had reached sexual maturity. "They discovered that great whites will always return to their birthing grounds when they are ready to find a partner. It would be a long road trip for nothing to cross the Pacific Ocean, to travel all the way to the northern shores of the Atlantic just to witness the sights."

"Maybe she got lost? What if you are wrong about her age?" Ellen didn't seem to buy Andy's story just yet.

"She's a big shark. I've watched her grow up around the island of Gansbaai for years. I'm not wrong about this. Look, the only way for sure is to check it out. As long as we can find her, we will make a scientific breakthrough. You have nothing to worry about."

Ellen stared forward at the back of the seat. "I hope you're right, for both of our sakes."

New York International Airport
New York City

Andy pushed his way through the crowd, doing his best to keep up with Ellen and her film crew. A jungle of people mobbed the food court of the terminal. They had a six-hour layover at the airport before their next departure and were keen to eat at a North American restaurant. Months of eating nothing but the local cuisine in South Africa had grown old; Andy craved a juicy burger and salty fries. His plan was to eat as much food as he could now and hopefully put himself into a food coma for the next five hours. The food court was enormous and had every type of cuisine you could ever want. There were local favorites, world-famous restaurants, and every fast-food chain imaginable. Thousands of people sat at tables, keeping to themselves as they devoured their food in a rush to catch their next flight. Ellen was already in line at Starbucks. Most of her crew had dissolved into the crowd and disappeared. Derrick was pacing back and forth between a pizza joint and a specialty bagel shop, the lineups getting longer and deeper as he struggled to decide.

The golden arches' yellow glow enticed Andy towards its counters, the long lineup moving swiftly. It didn't take long before Andy stood next in line, trying to decide what he wanted to get. "Good day, sir, how can I help you?" a young girl, no older than seventeen, said in a monotone voice. Her hair was a mess as it fell out from underneath her ball cap, the giant golden *M* faded.

"Yeah, I'll have the number three combo with large fries." Andy pointed up towards the menu hanging above the counter.

The girl didn't have to look up, instinctively punching in the meal. "Will that be all, sir?"

Andy tapped his fingers against the counter. "Better throw in a double cheeseburger and a shake." The server looked back up with a questioning look on her face. "And a ten box of nuggets with honey." The ebony skinned girl rang in the other items as quickly as Andy could rhyme them off. "Oh, and I should get a drink to wash it all down. Better throw in a coke."

"Mister, I'm glad I'm not sitting next to you on the jet," she snickered as she punched in his meal. "That will be $28.60."

Andy pulled out his wallet and took out a bundle of

South African currency. Each bill had the picture of an animal brilliantly coloured on it. "Shit, I knew I forgot to do something." Andy looked down at the girl. "You don't accept the rand here do you?"

"No, I'm sorry, sir." She poked her head into the kitchen and called out to one of the hidden employees. "Hold up on that last order." She walked back over to the counter with an awkward grin on her face. "Do you have any other way to pay, sir?"

Andy had left his debit card in his suitcase. He hadn't used it in months while working in the port of Gansbaai. "Derrick, come over here." Andy called out over the crowd.

"I just got in line." Derrick was standing in line, waiting for an authentic slice of New York pizza.

"Do you have your debit? I forgot mine in my luggage." Andy held up the colourful bills to show he didn't have a means of paying for his food.

Derrick hesitated to leave the line, but as soon as he did the next person eagerly took his place. "Here, use the tap, bring it back. I'll be at the back of that line." Derrick pointed to the New York Bagels line.

"I thought you were getting pizza?" Andy showed the young woman the debit card. She stuck her head back in the kitchen and signaled out for them to go ahead with the order.

"You ruined it for me. Now I want a bagel. Just don't forget to bring me back the card." Derrick rushed back to get in the line, nearly knocking over a man's tray as he zipped by.

Andy paid for his food and it didn't take long before it was ready. The server piled his food onto his tray, struggling to find room to fit it all onto the single trey. Andy secured his food with two hands, making sure he wouldn't spill anything as he walked through the packed food court. He walked over to Derrick, who was standing at the back of a thirty-person deep line. "Here you go, Derrick." Derrick reached out and stole a handful of fries. "Hey, man, get your own."

"Them's the rules, man. You order a large french fries you have to share. I didn't make them up." Derrick stuffed the fries in his mouth. "You don't like it, too bad. Should've brought your own card."

"Thanks, mate." Andy didn't mind sharing his fries with Derrick but knew he wouldn't be able to stand there much longer without losing more. He could see Derrick already eyeing his fries, so he decided he would leave now before it was too late. "I'll be over there if you ever get served." Andy watched a man gather the trash from the family's meal onto one tray, the universal signal you were getting ready to leave. He rushed over and waited next to the family as they stood up, grabbing a chair as soon as they were all stood up.

Andy slid his tray onto the table and took a long sip of his pop, the bubbles dancing on his tongue. He tore the wrapper off his cheeseburger and took a giant bite, getting a taste of everything in one mouthful. He tilted his head back and closed his eyes as he savored the flavours, trying to distinguish them as he chewed. Ketchup, cheese, mustard, pickles, onion, the toasted bun, and a charred all-beef patty. "I missed you."

"Jesus Christ, Andy, you must really miss American

food?" Ellen's voice startled him.

"Hey, you." He opened his eyes to see her sitting across from him with a coffee and wrap. "Hungry." He offered her the fries. Ellen reached over and grabbed the honey, tearing the lid off as she dunked a chicken nugget in. "Wow, you don't follow the rules of fast food?"

Ellen took a dainty bite of the chicken. "Can't say I ever have. Please explain." She dipped the nugget back into the sauce.

Andy shook his head. "My god, who raised you?"

"What?" Ellen looked confused.

"Well, for starters, you never double dip. Ever." Andy slid his tray closer to his chest. "And when someone offers you a fry, you can have a few, but you never just take a man's chicken nuggets." Andy tried his best to sound genuine, but his smile betrayed him.

Ellen laughed out loud, dimples formed on her cheeks as she smiled. "I've never heard of these rules before."

Derrick pulled out a chair and sat down, his plate had a cheese bagel toasted with cream cheese and a chocolate chip muffin with butter. "Andy, you didn't offer me a chicken nugget. I thought we were buddies?"

"You see what you started here." Andy held out the box as Derrick reached out and took one.

"Where's the honey?" Derrick asked. Ellen passed him the open pack.

Andy waited until Derrick dunked his chicken in the golden sauce. "She's a double dipper," Andy accused her

"You're not." Derrick seemed shocked, placing his nugget down on his trey. "You can't do that. Who raised you?"

Ellen laughed even harder. "Why didn't we have this much fun in South Africa?"

That was the question Andy was wondering. Maybe this break from the work was just what they all needed. They were all relaxed now, allowing themselves to joke around with each other a little more. It worried Andy that once they got to Newfoundland, if they didn't find the shark, Ellen would become distant again.

CHAPTER TEN

Labyrinth Oil Office
St. John's, Newfoundland

Kevin followed Lewis through the hallways of Labyrinth Oil. Expensive paintings hung on the walls by famous artists from all over the world. Most of them were abstract paintings which Kevin couldn't understand. He didn't agree that it was art, but there were millions of people who dished out hundreds of thousands of dollars for the mess. "Would you look at all of this art?" Kevin drew out the last word, trying to sound like a critic.

"I wouldn't call it art," Lewis said impatiently. "Isn't there supposed to be an elevator here somewhere?"

"The receptionist said it was at the end of this hallway." Kevin could sense that Lewis was nervous, especially after how the cops responded with laughter to his theory of a giant squid.

"We must be getting close now." Lewis quickened his pace. "I don't know why this needed to be done in person."

Kevin had told him that it was because that's how the Japanese did business, but he just wanted to have a reason to get close to Miss Eguchi. "It just does, Lewis. Nothing to worry about." The paintings on the wall were replaced by plaques and a trophy case, each one a major achievement for oil research and technological advances. The dark marble plaques had gold writing on them. The letters seemed to shine brightly, luring you in to read about why Labyrinth Oil was so great.

"Finally," Lewis grumbled as he pushed an onyx button on the wall. A chime beeped above, the digital display quickly descending from twenty all the way down to one. Two black doors with gold trim slid open to reveal a mirrored elevator. The two men stepped inside, and Lewis hit the button for the top floor.

"May I help you?" A voice came through the speaker.

"We are here to see Mr. Kurosawa," Lewis answered, taking charge before Kevin could answer.

"Do you have an appointment?"

Lewis looked at Kevin. "Do we have an appointment?"

Kevin shook his head. It had never crossed his mind to call ahead, but now he wished he had. "We are here on behalf of the Canadian Coast Guard. We have information about Mr. McGilvery." Kevin's years of experience allowed him to react quickly.

"Hold your issued identification cards up to the scanner."

Kevin took his ID card out of his wallet and held it underneath a card reader. Thin green lasers scanned the card. After a few silent moments the elevator started its ascent. "Looks like we solved the problem."

"Thanks." Lewis looked at his reflection in the mirrored wall. He brushed back the stray strand of hair and fixed the collar of his shirt.

"Just relax, Lewis." Kevin looked at his own reflection, fixing his shirt to hide his gut as much as possible. He pulled up his pants, trying to hide the bulging roll of fat hanging over his belt. The elevator doors pulled apart with a loud swooshing sound, opening into Mr. Kurosawa's private office. The far wall was a floor-to-ceiling window, giving a breath-taking view of St. John's Harbour. Mr. Kurosawa sat behind a giant slab of mahogany wood, a large bookshelf teeming with texts to his right.

"Good day, gentleman." Mr. Kurosawa stood up, buttoning his dress jacket in the process before walking over to greet his guest.

"Good day, Mr. Kurosawa." Lewis's voice was strong and confident. "I am Lewis Park and this is my boss, Kevin O'Reilly."

Mr. Kurosawa bowed his head. "How can I be of help today?" His English was strong, but you could pick up his Japanese heritage on certain words.

"Well, sir, we are from the Canadian Coast guard and we wanted to come see you about your boss, Mr. McGilvery." Lewis said politely.

"Please, come have a seat." Mr. Kurosawa walked back behind the oversized desk and sat in his leather chair.

Kevin sat down, sinking comfortably into the cushion. Lewis sat next to him and the three men shared a long, awkward silence. Mr. Kurosawa combed his jet-black hair straight back; his gel gave it a sleek shimmer. His pinstripe grey suit vest was left unbuttoned. A silver clip held his pale pink tie in place.

"Thanks for having us on such short notice, Mr. Kurosawa." Lewis sat with perfect posture, his large frame dwarfing the man sitting across from him.

"Please, you can call me Kal."

"So, will Miss Eguchi be joining us?" Kevin asked. Lewis shot him an angry glare, his eyes widening with rage.

"No, my sister-in-law will not be joining us." Kal's voice was sharp. "Should she be here?"

"I'm sorry, Mr. Kurosawa. I think Kevin just wanted her here because of any legal problems that may arise." Lewis's statement seemed to defuse the situation.

"Yeah, I mean if you have to file a missing person's report under suspicious circumstances." Kevin's tongue tripped over his words. He could barely form a complete sentence. "I think this situation needs to be handled with the utmost care."

"I will pass along any information that will apply to the report." Kal leaned forward in his chair and placed his hands on the table. They were balled into fists now. "Now, please, I'm a very busy man in Mr. McGilvery's absence."

"We believe Mr. McGilvery may have met an untimely death. His body was nowhere to be found, and we found blood all over the cabin of his yacht." Lewis spoke clearly but quickly. "Did Mr. McGilvery have any known enemies?"

"Jonah did not make many friends during his time here. Many of the fisherman wanted him gone, but that's nothing new for Mr. McGilvery. Being the owner of a major oil corporation afforded him few friends and a wealth of enemies." Kal's dark chestnut eyes glared at Kevin suspiciously. "I believe you were at the press conference yesterday morning with the mob of fishermen."

Kevin lowered his eyes to glance at the floor. "I was there, but I wasn't with the fishermen. I was just there wasting time before work began." Kevin continued to stare at the floor boards, admiring the red oak. Dark swirls ran through the hardwood creating an intricate pattern that screamed wealth.

"I see. I've been in contact with a Detective Bowers. He believes a fisherman from Marystown may be responsible for Jonah's death."

"Did he say why?" Kevin blurted out.

Kal eyed Kevin suspiciously. "Said he got a phone call from an anonymous source."

"There is another thing I found." Lewis hesitated; his hand clutched the plastic bag that was tucked away in his pants pocket. He pulled the tooth out and laid it on the table. "I found this embedded in the decking of the *Swift Current.*"

Kal reached out and pulled the tooth inches away from his face, running his index finger over the ragged edge. He looked at it intently from different angles. "This tooth belongs to a kraken."

"A kraken?" Kevin asked.

"Growing up, my father told me tales of an ancient sea monster called a kraken." Kal placed his hands in his lap and leaned back in his chair. "My father told me tales of the giant squid. They would drag ships to the bottom of the ocean and devour the unfortunate crew."

"Someone told me this belong to the *Architeuthis dux.*"

Lewis remembered the name that Kate used.

"Arc a tooth us what?" Kevin felt left out of the conversation. Apparently the two men were speaking a different language.

"A giant squid, Kevin." Lewis was growing annoyed with him. "I believe those creatures are common around the waters of the Grand Banks," he added.

Kal nodded his head in agreement. "Yes, they are. We've had several ecological surveys done in the area and they are abundant, but we determined them to be harmless. I have workers getting ready to dive into those waters to get the pipeline laid. They will be down there for months. Labyrinth Oil cannot afford to have any more bad publicity come from this project. We are having a hard enough time dealing with the fishermen's union."

"What are you going to do about it?" Kevin asked, drawing the ire of Kal, his eyes flaring with anger.

"That is none of your concern." Kal stood up and buttoned up his vest. "Now, is there anything else we should know?"

Lewis shook his head. "No, sir, that is everything we needed to tell you."

"Then I must ask you two gentlemen to leave. I have a lot of work to do, so if you'd excuse me." Kal waved them back toward the elevator.

Kevin stood up first and turned to leave, not waiting for Lewis. The door opened as soon as he touched the button. He slipped inside and did his best to hide.

Lewis wasn't far behind. He lumbered into the confined space and waited for the door to close behind him. "What the fuck is wrong with you, Kevin?"

"Whoa, calm down, Lewis." Kevin wasn't about to take shit from Lewis.

Lewis paced back and forth, his face flushing red. "You really made us look stupid back there. I mean, what the hell was that? Why the hell did you ask about Miss Eguchi."

"That's enough out of you. It's over for us. We have nothing else to do with this now." Kevin ignored Lewis's questions. "The police will handle the matter now, and we will go back to patrolling the waters for the coast guard. End of conversation." The elevator beeped as the door slid open. Both men tried to push through the door at the same time. Lewis easily pushed Kevin back, shoving him deeper into the elevator as he stormed off through the lobby and out the front door.

7 Colonial Street
St. John's, NL
Kevin O'Reilly's home

Cramped in between the wall and the dining room table, Kevin's stomach pressed hard against the edge. One side of the dinner table had become ingrained into the drywall, the oversized table wedged into a small alcove just off the kitchen. It was a stretch calling it a dining room; it was just the place that his wife decided they would dine in. The cheap table was just big enough for the cramped space and it forced the married couple to stare at each other uncomfortably. Kevin enjoyed the sweet scent of apples in Amy's cinnamon coloured hair that hung in tight curls around her round face. Amy was dressed casually, wearing jeans and a hipster jacket pulled on over a blue dress shirt. Kevin looked at his own reflection, jealous over how little time had transformed her beauty while father time seemed to have declared war on him. Amy always had a shyness to her, a reluctance to show off her exceptional looks which is why it still shocked him to this day she had cheated on him. A picture of her son hung on a frame behind her, a perpetual reminder of her unfaithfulness. The ceiling tiles were old and sagged down in the center. A bare bulb hung from the ceiling. Kevin had broken the shade a month ago while changing the light bulb and hadn't bothered to replace it since. A narrow window with the drapes hanging down just above the windowsill offered a view of the neighbours' siding

Kevin stared down at his plate. The food didn't look appetizing and the portions were small. The batter on his fried cod looked wet. The steamed vegetables looked soggy and their vibrant colours had left with the steam. He scrapped his fork over his plate in disgust, wishing he had ate before he came home. At least he had grabbed a beer from the fridge before he sat down to his dinner. He picked up the brown bottle and took a long swig. Amy shot him a warning glare from across the table. Placing the bottle of Black Horse back down on the table, Kevin reached out for the salt and pepper, dusting an unhealthy portion of both over his fried fish. They ate in silence for what seemed like an eternity. Kevin reached for the television remote and flicked on the news. He needed something to distract him from Amy's look of disdain.

"I thought we agreed no television during supper?" Amy spoke in a disheartened tone.

"I want to hear the news, Amy. Is that all right?" Kevin

let out a long sigh. Amy just glared at him with her deep blue eyes. He couldn't see the screen, but the sound was enough to distract him from his bland meal.

"*So, you're saying that global warming has reached its apex?*" a male reporter asked.

"*What I'm trying to say,*" a woman's voice explained in a soft tone. "*We've already tipped the scale too far. There's no reversing the damage we've done now.*"

"*What effects will this have, Miss Northcott?*"

"He can't be serious?" Amy mocked the interview.

Kevin pointed his fork at Amy. "Hey, I thought you said no television during dinner," Kevin said playfully, trying his best to connect on some level with her. Amy leaned towards the living room, listening to the answer as she cracked a smile.

"*We've already experienced nasty storms around the world. The worst and most frequent storms have been happening off the coast of Newfoundland. The waves have pounded the shoreline with so much force they've registered on the seismometer. These storms are only the beginning. We will soon feel a drastic change in the world's temperatures. There will be an increase in natural disasters such as earthquakes, typhoons, hurricanes, tornados, and drastic flooding. That's when the real dangerous activity will start.*"

"*Would you explain to the viewers what could happen, Madeline?*"

"*I believe that we will soon witness a drastic increase in the movements of the tectonic plates. There will be powerful actions where the plates converge and diverge. This will cause a drastic change in the structure of the continents and land masses all over the world.*"

"Is there anything we can do to stop this?"

"We can't stop it. We've set the earth on this course. All we can do now is adjust our actions so these effects won't last as long and hope we can survive through this ordeal. We need to stop using fossil fuels all together. Companies like Labyrinth Oil must be stopped immediately."

"That was a recording from earlier today in Washington at an emergency meeting about global warming. We will be back after the commercial break with the local news and the latest update on the Jonah McGilvery case."

"What a pile of crap," Kevin muttered.

Amy stared at him with blank eyes. "You must be blind if you can't see the effects of global warming all around us."

"It's the way the world works, Amy." Kevin took another sip of his beer, immediately regretting where the conversation was heading.

"But working out on the ocean you must see the terrible storms that woman was talking about," Amy said.

"Butts are for crapping, Amy," Kevin stood up from the table. His gut bumped the side causing the frail legs to wobble underneath. He walked over to the fridge and grabbed another beer. "I'll be in the living room." Kevin slumped down into his rocking chair, leaving Amy to clear the table and wash the dishes.

CHAPTER ELEVEN

Placentia Bay
Southern Coast of Newfoundland
The Mississippi

Peter Breau sat on the edge of his twelve-foot yacht with the air regulator piece pressed hard against his face, building up the courage to go spear fishing. The weight of his oxygen tank was drawing the straps deep down into his shoulder. The vivid yellow sun beat down on his balding head, scorching his scalp. Beads of perspiration rolled down his backside and formed a puddle in his Kevlar wetsuit. He found it tough to concentrate with the blaring heavy metal music pounding from the cabin of the *Mississippi*. Peter felt the deck of the new fishing boat vibrating underneath his feet as the base boomed.

The last time he went spear fishing was ten years ago in Costa Rica, and the waters were much warmer than in Placentia Bay. He decided he needed a break from the hectic city life, and began looking for a place to clear his writers' block. Ever since he sold his script to those damn television producers, he hadn't been able to get a single word out of his head and onto paper. He was lucky he had enough material written to stretch his show out over two seasons, but the first season had already aired and the network was hungry for more. Peter had to stimulate his brain. His only plan had been to take the ferry over from North Sydney and charter a car in Port aux Basques. Since then, he had been taking in all of what Newfoundland offered. He was trying to discover adventure, which led him all the way to Placentia. Now, as a struggling young fisherman blasted a heavy metal tune over his sound system, Peter was preparing to make the plunge into the ocean. The speargun clutched tightly in his grasp, Peter kept looking over his shoulder into the bleak waters.

"Please tell me there aren't many sharks out here?" Peter questioned his tour guide.

Looking up from behind the steering wheel, the young fisherman turned the music down just enough, allowing his voice to be heard over the obnoxiously loud music. "You might see a porbeagle, but I doubt it." The words escaped his mouth rapidly, weighed down by a thick accent. The captain had pulled his yellow hip waders over a stained white T-shirt. Long strands of curly brown hair fell over his eyes, and it looked like he hadn't washed it in days. Peter stared at the grime built up on his palms and underneath his fingernails as the fisherman lowered a rope over the side of the *Mississippi*.

"What is a porbeagle?" Peter asked, wondering why he was sitting on the edge of this boat. He should be seated in front of his computer writing the scripts for the third season. He looked down at seventeen notifications on his phone, all from the network producers looking for any progress from him. Peter never expected for his script to take off, but the overwhelming ratings demanded more.

"It's a smaller shark. Notting to worry bout, mate."

Peter wondered if the young man was putting on an act. This time his accent sounded Australian. "How often do people report shark attacks around here?"

The fisherman scratched his head with a confused look on his face. "I can't recall there ever being a reported shark attack in these waters here." He paused as if searching a database for the correct file. "Can't say I ever did."

A wave sent a spray of frigid water up Peter's back. Droplets streaked through the neck hole of his wetsuit, following the zipper all the way down to his crotch. He recoiled into a tight ball at the sensation. He hadn't realized how hot the sun was until the frigid ocean water splashed against his bare skin. Peter let out a surprised whimper, arching his back trying to escape the icy water inside his suit. The fisherman let out a genuine chuckle at Peter, enjoying his rigid reaction to the numbing waters of Newfoundland. "Anything else I need to know?" Peter asked.

"The waters round here aren't too deep, but you will want to keep an eye on yer air gauge." The fisherman reached out to the gauge on Peter's wetsuit. "You'll want to make yer way back up once this red needle reaches thirty." He patted Peter's shoulders with calloused hands. "You'll be fine, don't you worry bout nottin."

"What's your name again?" Peter had been so nervous preparing to get into the water, he was drawing a blank trying to remember his name.

"You can call me Felix."

Peter nodded before pulling the mask over his face

and securing the regulator in place. He took a few steady breaths before giving Felix a thumbs up. He leaned back slightly, letting the weight of his oxygen tank do most of the work for him. Peter fell backwards off the side of the *Mississippi* and plunged into the freezing cold waters of Placentia Bay. His muscles constricted as the shock took hold of his body, his vision blurred by a massive swarm of air bubbles. For what seemed like an eternity, Peter sank deeper into the ocean helpless to defend himself against any predators. All he was able to detect was the booming vibrations coming from the music aboard the *Mississippi*, the thumping drumbeat echoing all around him.

The last air bubbles drifted past Peter's mask and floated away, allowing him a breathtaking view of the ocean floor. Years of erosion and sediment covered it in jagged rock formations. Seaweed and lobsters swayed back and forth with the strong current. Peter quickly adapted to the water temperature and rapidly pumped his legs, propelling himself downwards, deeper into the abyss. He looked back towards the surface. The sunlight struggled to penetrate the immense darkness of the ocean and reach the bottom. He looked around as a codfish swam past him and scurried off out of sight. Peter continued to dive deeper into unknown waters of Placentia Bay, completely cut off from all of his troubles for a brief moment.

Placentia Bay
Southern Coast of Newfoundland
One-hundred Metres Down

Joan swept her nose back and forth, sketching a picture of the ocean depths with pinpoint accuracy. She could sense the other male great whites around her. They had been pursuing her now for days. Every time she waded into the shallow waters around the coastline, she could sense the warmer waters changing her attitude. She moved faster near the surface and her muscles swelled with power, but with the newfound energy she required more fuel. Her stomach rumbled for sustenance as she continued her journey along the southern coast of the island, doing her best to remain ahead of the males seeking to mate with her.

A constant throb of electronic impulses echoed in the distance unlike anything Joan had ever heard. Felix had turned up his heavy metal music after Peter made his dive, and it taunted the prehistoric predator, daring her to investigate. Steady vibrations and constant thumping of the bass drum annoyed the shark, drawing her full attention. The foreign noise made it impossible to ignore; she had to find out what was causing the disturbance. Her brain's capacity to focus on a single source allowed her to ignore all the other distractions. She swam swiftly towards the source of the disturbance, raising up from the depths of the dark ocean to get a better idea of what was drawing her towards the surface. The *Carcharodon* sensed the familiar humming of a boat's engine entangled with the unknown sound. Joan kept her distance from the pounding source of electrical impulses that stimulated her lateral lines. Until she knew what kind of creature waited for her, she remained in the shadows of the murky water.

With her appetite growing stronger, her killer instincts took over, making her desperate for a meal. Her heart pumped blood through her veins, strengthening her muscles for an ambush if she discovered any prey to devour, anything able to keep her going until her next meal. She sensed the other white sharks closing in on the area, momentarily ignoring the hormones that Joan excreted. Whatever was making the commotion, it was considerably larger than the other predators in these waters, emitting powerful impulses throughout the ocean. Joan felt the beating hearts of the *Architeuthis dux* and the flutter of whales making their migration south from the Arctic sea. If the origin of the noise wasn't food, her ability to quickly locate her next meal allowed her the luxury to investigate. For the moment, the boisterous noise drew her attention towards *the Mississippi*.

Placentia Bay
Southern Coast of Newfoundland
Forty Metres Down

A freezing cold current of water marked the boundary of the drop-off. Peter looked off into the ominous blackness of the uncharted depths, a chill creeping up his spine. He wouldn't dare venture past the ocean floor that he could still see. The waters turned so dark they looked purple as the trickle of sunlight died in the depths on the other side of the cliff. Peter had followed a three-foot codfish for about twenty minutes now, the dark silver scales picking up slivers of fading sunlight as it swam near the ocean floor. He grasped his speargun in his hands now, making certain he secured the cable to his wrist. The ocean floor was teaming with crustaceans swaying back and forth with the strong currents. He could see an assortment of lobsters picking apart a cluster of starfish, stuffing morsels of flesh into their mouths with their claws. Peter had never seen so much activity underneath the water before. It was fascinating to watch. Years of gloom shrouded the rugged sea bed in algae. The remnants of wrecked ships littered about the ocean floor, left well preserved over the ages.

Peter checked his air gauge and his heart plummeted in his rib cage, disheartened to find it had dropped to forty percent. He had to make his move before he would have to return to the surface. He forced his legs to kick hard, churning up a barrage of air bubbles that drifted towards the surface behind him. The codfish banked hard to the left and then left again, attracted by the commotion that Peter was causing. The fish swam close enough for Peter to line up his shot, but it swam by him too quickly, passing him before he could pull the trigger. Peter twisted his body and took quick aim, squeezing the trigger before the codfish disappeared from view.

A low thump from the speargun echoed through the water as the spear pierced through the codfish's soft flesh. A faint mist of red blood trickled from the wound, clouding the fish from his view. Peter pulled the line in, hand over hand. The fish moved in jerky motions through the deep waters, leaving a trail of blood behind. Peter reached out and snatched the fish by the gills, drawing it in towards his body. He didn't want to lose his kill, but he didn't think he'd be able to get much flesh to eat.

A massive grey blur formed in the distance, appearing from nowhere like a ghost. The grey blur raced towards Peter, drawn in by the trail of blood. Fear gripped Peter's heart so hard that it ceased pumping, every muscle in his body tightened so taut it hurt. A sinister grin took shape as the grey blur came into focus. Before Peter realized what was happening, the grin opened wide, revealing an avalanche of razor-sharp teeth and pink gums. A black hole opened wide as the creature's jaws widened. Peter tried to swim away but was pulled inwards by the engulfing water. Raising his arm out of instinct, Peter tried to block the blow, but his efforts did little to stop the impact. A wallop more powerful than a freight train crashed into his chest. The shark slammed into him with its eight-thousand pound body. Three-inch teeth severed the human flesh with ease. An immense pressure washed over Peter as the jaw slammed shut with over four-thousand pounds of pressure per square inch. A crimson cloud engulfed Peter. He felt the pressure increase as the shark swam into the depths with tremendous speed. Peter's body quivered. His heart leapt into his chest as he found himself still alive but trapped in the creature's gullet. The creature opened his jaw and Peter's eyes focused on his own severed arm floating upwards, his fingers still clutching the speargun. With a jerking motion, the sharks jaw unhinged and jutted forward, its teeth tearing through Peter's flesh. For an abrupt moment, the creature relinquished Peter from its gnarled jaw. A soulless eye peered back at him. His mind trapped inside his mangled body; Peter was forced to witness slivers of his own shredded flesh stuck in the rows of razor-sharp teeth.

Peter found himself face to face with the pitch-black eye. Frozen in time, he saw flashes of his family playing on the creature's eye like an old projector movie. Loving memories played, images of Kelli, Dante, and Jaden flicked across the dark pupil. Peter was filled with a fleeting sense of happiness as the memory of his loved ones raced through his mind. Without warning, the movie ended abruptly. The black eyes rolled back into the creature's skull and its jaws hyper-extended without warning. An exploding shower of red burst into the sea as the jaws snapped shut over Peter's chest and neck.

Placentia Bay
Southern Coast of Newfoundland
The Mississippi

The bass drum pounded loudly as Felix leaned back in his comfy chair, pretending to play along to the beat of the song with his pencil in the air. Loud music drowned out the cawing of the seagulls and turrs. The song ended, and for a brief moment all Felix heard was the gentle sound of waves lapping off the side of the *Mississippi*. Sharp, piercing cries of seagulls overhead caught his attention. He watched the dirty white birds circling above his boat through the filthy windshield.

Thump thump thump thump

A rhythmic thumping caught his attention just before the next song kicked in. Felix sat up in his chair as something bumped against the hull of the ship. He reached out to his CD player and turned the volume down.

Thump thump thump thump

The rhythmic sound returned, and it only took Felix a moment to realize the waves had washed something up against the side of the boat. He got up from his chair and headed out onto the deck. He placed both hands on the metal railing that ran along the port side of his vessel and looked out into the vast horizon of the ocean. The deep blue sea met the light blue sky in tranquil transition.

Thump   thump   thump   thump

Felix looked down into the waves, and it didn't take him long to spot the source of the sound. His stomach muscles convulsed, sending the contents of his tuna sandwich over the side of the rail. The vomit splattering off the water with a sickening sound. Felix wiped the half-digested food mush from his mouth and stared down at the chunk of arm severed just above the elbow. The ghostly white hand still clutched the spear gun as it bobbed up and down in the water with the waves.

CHAPTER TWELVE

The Marine Institute
St. John's, NL

Kate sat behind her desk with the door to the class-room closed, eating her lunch as she skimmed through her emails. There was nothing there except emails from her students pleading for an extension on their home-work, or why they wouldn't be able to attend class on Monday. Stabbing a piece of hard-boiled egg with her fork, Kate frowned at the greenish colour of the yolk as she nudged the plastic tray aside. She anxiously await-ed an email from the lab; they were supposed to let her know as soon as the shark carcass found in Logy Bay ar-rived. She needed to identify the species and determine the cause of death. Sharks had never been in her scope of expertise, or even something she was familiar with, but marine biology was her chosen discipline. Excited for the challenge and a break from teaching, this recent discovery would be a welcome change.

She opened her internet browser and searched for an expert in the field. Kate planned to document her find-ings, and if she encountered any problems, she would quickly contact a paleobiologist. She searched through all the names, many of them associated with other universities. Most of the experts listed lived in California, South Africa, and New Zealand. As Kate scrolled past Andy Grant's name, his picture caught her attention. His deep brown eyes drew her in, and his chestnut brown hair paired perfectly with his five o'clock shadow. Everyone had seen his show on television during shark week, and Kate still found it hard to believe his biography. He certainly did not act like someone that had their master's degree in paleobiology. She had always thought they had hired him because he was attractive, just an actor paid to play the part.

She jotted down his contact info for his office at the University of California and decided this may be a great opportunity to reach out to him. Without hesitation, Kate opened her email. Her fingers wandered across the keyboard. Her heart fluttered in her chest, and she felt her face flush with blood. The mouse hovered over the send button, her eyes reading the request for help to identify the shark making sure it was written professionally. Kate closed her eyes as her finger clicked the mouse. A bell chimed instantly alerting her that the email had been delivered successfully. Almost instantaneously, an email popped up on her dashboard from him.

"Damn it." Kate stared at the automatic reply, disheartened to discover he was presently in South Africa.

"Kate, we have the specimen down in the lab if you want to come look." Danielle startled Kate. She was in charge of the tanks in the basement, making sure she kept the salinity of the water at the proper levels for all the marine life. Her job was vital for keeping all the different species alive so that the institution could examine them.

"Thanks, Danielle, I'll be down once I'm finished reading this email." Kate closed her internet browser and powered off her laptop.

The Marine Institute
St. John's, NL

Kate walked into the visitors' section of the university. Tours ran through the basement daily between lunch and supper. They were the best source of income for the school because it was both an opportunity to educate and inspire young people, but it also served as an effective tool in teaching students. Students would practice what they learned in the classroom by answering the questions that would get brought up during the tours. There were interactive displays where people could learn about how the ocean tide worked and how the moon affected it. Kids could control the moon with a lever which would allow more or less water into the tank to show how the tides affected the landscape. There were three rooms that played movies about the various marine life found in the oceans around Newfoundland and Labrador. The biggest attractions were the fossilized displays of various fish found off the coast. The biggest display was the skeleton of a blue whale that had been reconstructed and hung from the ceiling, the massive fragments of bone held together with metal rods and screws. A tank with a preserved juvenile *Architeuthis dux* ran the length of one wall; its giant eye seemed to watch you wherever you went through the yellowed water.

They kept the basement of the Marine Institute extra cold to help stabilize the water temperatures. Large steel drums lined the back walls and water from the salt water tanks wet the cement floors. Each tank containing different marine life. They filled one with lobsters and crabs. If you looked closely enough you would be able to find the blue lobster donated by a local fisherman. Codfish swam in the largest tank and a net was thrown over the tank containing the wolffish so visitors wouldn't be able to get their hands close enough to the water. Someone had nicknamed the Atlantic wolffish the devil fish for good reason. Its jaws were filled with fang-like, conical teeth which it used to break the shells of molluscs and crustaceans. The final tank housed starfish, sea snails, and other fish which children could touch. Kate walked straight past those tanks and towards a door that led out back. A large yellow sign with red dashes warned visitors to stay out. The words *restricted access* scrolled across the sign in bold black letters. She pushed the heavy door open. A blast of ice-cold air carrying the heavy scent of salt and algae greeted her. They housed the filtration systems for all of the tanks in this area along with all the large display tanks that housed various species of fish not on display for the public.

"Over here, Kate." Danielle's voice carried over the hum of the pumps as they filtered water through the pipes. She was standing next to a large blue tarp that had been wrapped over the body of the deceased shark. She waved for two of her students to come over. The two young men and Danielle struggled to roll the dead weight enough to get the tarp out from underneath the one-thousand-pound shark.

Kate rushed over to help. The stench from the inside the tarp burned the hairs in her nose. It smelled like rotten salt and ammonia, something Kate never would have dreamed of before today. Straining all of her muscles to help, she felt the incredible weight of the powerful sea creature roll over. The students pulled the tarp away once the weight shifted then stood behind Kate and Danielle to observe. The shark had a long slit that ran the length of its belly, but, miraculously, the contents of its guts remained inside. "Well, it's a male shark." Kate pointed towards two appendages hanging from the white belly. "We call those two organs claspers," she explained for the two students. Kate examined the pectoral and dorsal fins for any signs of damage. "It's a young shark, very young as a matter of fact."

"Why would you say that?" Danielle asked as she reached down to touch the skin. She recoiled in pain instantly as she tried to rub the creatures grey back. "What the hell?" Danielle's hand was bleeding from a nasty looking cut. She took a rag out of her pocket and applied pressure to the cut. "I'll go get a band aid."

"A shark's skin is made of dermal denticles woven together." Kate continued to explain to Danielle's students. "They act like armour and help to keep its skin clean. If you rub them the wrong way, the denticles will shred your flesh, but if you rub from snout to tail like this." Kate reached down and ran her hand along the sharks back without incident. "It's smooth. Give it a try."

The two young men hesitantly reached their hands out, afraid to touch the dead creature. "Don't be afraid, guys. She just showed you that it's safe." Danielle was back now with a ball of gauze taped to her hand. "I wish you had shown me before."

"Sorry, I thought it was common knowledge." Kate said bashfully.

"Anyway, you said that this is a young shark." Danielle made a fist with her hand, squeezing the wad of gauze. "Could you please explain that to us?"

"As I was saying." Kate pointed to the perfect dorsal fin. "You notice that the dorsal fin is almost a perfect triangle. As sharks grow older, they will encounter other sharks and predators, often they will fight each other to assert dominance. As they grow older, they will be involved in more of these confrontations. An older shark will have more battle scars on average than their younger counterparts. We can use the wounds and scratches on a shark's dorsal fin to identify the creature similarly to how we can identify each other using finger prints. Each dorsal fin is unique."

"Seriously? Like a finger print?" Danielle's lips curled up and wrinkles formed on her forehead as her eyebrows scrunched together.

"Yes." Kate moved towards the snout. "See these black marks that pepper its pyramid-shaped head. These are the ampullae of Lorenzini."

"I've heard of those. That is how sharks detect electrical impulses, right?" Danielle interrupted.

"That is correct. They can also detect the smallest amount of blood or urine in the ocean waters from extremely far distances. Thousands of metres away."

"That's incredible," Danielle added as she nodded her head in amazement. "So, what kind of shark do you think this is then?"

"I think it could be a great white shark." Kate found it hard to believe that she said that, but she was almost positive it was. "I must run tests on it. I'll need blood and skin samples before I can confirm. Do you think you could arrange your students to gather that for me?"

"Of course, Doctor Hamilton." One student was eager to help now.

"So, what could have caused the wound on its stomach?" Danielle asked.

"I don't understand." Kate had seen nothing like it. The cut had been made with surgical precision, clean as if made by the skilled and steady hand of a surgeon. "I think I need to make a phone call." Kate tried to get hold of someone in Andy Grant's office. Hopefully he would be excited to hear about the discovery of a *Carcharodon carcharias* in Newfoundland.

St. John's International Airport
St. John's, NL

Andy had fallen asleep during the last leg of the plane trip to Newfoundland during the in-flight movie. The steward had woken him up to buckle up his seat belt. He awoke in a dazed and confused state, forgetting momentarily where he was or where he was headed. He wiped the drool from the corner of his mouth, bumping elbows with the passenger next to him. The flight was crowded, and Andy had lost sight of Ellen a long time ago. Derrick was just two rows ahead of him, towering over everyone around him. His hair had grown long in the back and was straggly looking. The seat belt light was lit up, and they had turned the lights back on while Andy had fallen asleep.

He looked at the elderly gentleman sitting next to him. His snow-white hair was nearing the end of its life cycles as he was closing in on baldness. The dome light on the top of his head reflected off of his scalp underneath his thin hair. "I hope I didn't keep you up with my snoring," Andy said.

The elderly man shot him a vexed look; his eyes circled by two large dark ellipses from lack of sleep. "It wasn't only me son," he said with a gruff tone.

"Sorry." Andy's voice trailed off. He didn't know what else to say, but it wouldn't be much longer before they'd be off this plane. He could already feel the plane descending. His stomach seemed to be behind the plane's altitude. With every drop, the bile in his stomach sloshed around inside his empty gut. He grabbed hold of the barf bag tucked into the pouch on the back of the seat in front of him. He opened it and put his face down into the bag, waiting for the next drop in altitude. Normally he didn't get sick, but the strong winds had created a lot of turbulence, and now there seemed to be big pockets of air that the plane was diving into.

A sudden drop caused the bile to jump into his throat as the plane leveled out. The acidic fluids drained back down into his gut. "Come on, buddy, land this plane." Andy didn't want to throw up; he had way too much in his stomach for the tiny white bag he was clutching. Looking around at the other passengers, Andy noticed he wasn't the only one that found the flight a little too turbulent. Several people had their heads between their knees.

The plane's landing gear was grinding below his seat, the mechanical arms of the wheel shifting around beneath the floor.

Another drop rattled the contents of his stomach, swishing around his insides. This time his lungs expanded against his rib cage as he held his breath and waited for the nausea to pass. Andy dry heaved, hoping to relieve some pressure building up inside, but it was no use. He looked out of the window but only a thick grey fog was visible. Beads of moisture ran across the window as the plane descended through the low ceiling. Not only was Andy sick to his stomach, now a wave of claustrophobia washed over him too. He didn't understand how the pilot guided the plane down towards the runway without being able to see. The pilot was only relying on his navigational instruments to guide the plane to safety. Blood drained from Andy's face. He looked down at the skin on his hands which were now pasty white. Beads of sweat dripped down his forehead and soaked into his beard, making the hairs prickly and sore.

A sudden rumble rattled the luggage compartments overhead as the wheels struck the ground. The whole plane shook as the breaks strained to slow the plane. Andy peered out the window once more, the yellow reflective paint scarcely visible on the runway. The immense fog seemed to swallow up everything on the ground. The terminal was ten feet away and was half shrouded by the sheer density of the grey mist. The plane's engine rumble faded as the twin turbine engines powered down, the plane slowly plodding down the tarmac.

"You made it." The elderly gentleman mocked him.

"First time to Newfoundland, I guess. Most days are like this. You get used to it after time."

"I don't think I ever want to get used to that sensation." Now that Andy knew he was safely on the ground the blood slowly returned to his body, and the urge to vomit passed. Andy waited for the man to grab his stuff from the overhead compartment, taking a moment to gather his strength before standing. "Sorry I wasn't much company during the flight." The elderly man slung a satchel over his shoulder, giving Andy one last glance before sauntering down the aisle with the rest of the passengers. Andy noticed Derrick waving people past his seat as he waited. He looked around for Ellen, but she had vanished into the crowd as they shuffled off the plane. Andy was the last one to leave. His knees wobbled underneath him as made his way towards Derrick.

"We got a phone call from the office. They need you to check something out for them." Derrick held his cellphone in his hands. The tiny black phone looked like a child's toy in his giant paws.

"We don't have time for that. We need to check Joan's tracker and find her before it's too late." Andy clutched the seat in front of him as he stumbled past Derrick.

"They want us to head to the St. John's Marine institute." Derrick joined Andy in the aisle. "They think they found a juvenile great white. Doctor Kate Hamilton wants us to check it out."

"I will join her with the film crew. It will thrill Ellen to get footage of a great white shark here in Newfoundland." Andy could feel his heart beating faster with excitement. "You take the rest of the crew and get that satellite tag tracker working and charter us a boat so we can get out there and find Joan of Shark."

"Now joining us live from Signal Hill is Jody Baker."

Andy looked up at the television on the terminal wall as the local news played. Everyone had stopped to watch the report. As the camera panned over the blue ocean, a wall of fog rolled in towards land. The blonde-haired and blue-eyed reporter was wearing a light blue windbreaker. Strong gusts of wind blew her hair completely sideways, her coat ready to blow away with the wind as it pulled tight against her slender body.

"Thanks, Micheal. The waters off Newfoundland have always been considered by many to be treacherous, but now in the last three days two people have gone missing somewhere out here." The camera panned away to some footage from earlier of a news conference. A police officer was taking questions from behind a podium. *"Yes, Mr. Breau's arm turned up at the surface of the water but we could not find his body."* The officer leaned in as one reporter asked a question that Andy couldn't hear over the murmur of the airport crowd. *"No, we do not believe this case to be related to Mr. McGilvery's case. I realize that they have both disappeared under mysterious circumstances, but I don't believe we are looking for a serial killer. The two men have no known ties to each other. Next question."* A voice called out from the crowd. *"We believe someone has murdered Mr. McGilvery, but we are exploring other avenues of investigation."*

An outburst of chatter erupted from the crowd as people added their two cents to the situation. Some people sympathized with the man's situation while others agreed he had it coming. The television switched to a long shot of a fishing boat named the *Mississippi*. Then it showed a stock photo of Peter Breau on the screen before it changed to an interview with the captain of the fishing vessel. *"I heard a strange knocking against the side of the boat. When I looked over all I could see was his arm just floating there. That's all we managed to find."* The screen switched back to a live shot of Jody Baker. *"Police officers have said Mr. McGilvery's yacht the Swift Current was found, and there were signs of a struggle aboard. However, they have yet to find his body. As for Mr. Breau, all they have found was his severed arm, but an autopsy is being conducted now to find the cause of the wound. Back to you, Micheal."* The report went back to the studio. *"Thanks, Jody. We will be back after this commercial break."*

Andy wandered towards the luggage coral, waiting for his suitcase to come out on the track. There was definitely something happening off the coast of Newfoundland, but he wasn't sure what it was yet.

CHAPTER THIRTEEN

Atlantic Ocean
Cliffs of the Grand Banks

A bull humpback whale breached the surface, sending a sprout of sea water gushing from its blowhole. The massive, solitary whale was following the migration path south, chasing the capelin before they moved on to breed. The baleen whale was a brute, measuring just over fifty-feet long and topping the scales at over thirty metric tonnes. He had been around for eighty years now, and he had become adept at putting on layers of thick blubber that would sustain him during the warmer weather. Its giant head and lower jaw were covered with tubercles, giving it a bumpy look. Slapping the surface of the water with its fluke tail, the bull dove back into the deeper waters. The giant mammal sang a complex song, calling out to the other members of his species, warning them to stay away from his meal. The humpback pumped its tail and raced towards the capelin, getting ready to to feast upon thousands of the small fish. Whales would not eat once it reached the warmer waters, and it needed to make sure it had enough blubber to last him a long time. Once the mating ritual was over, he would gorge himself in the nutrient-rich waters of the Caribbean before making his migration back north.

The whale could sense a threat lurking in the depths, watching him from down below. Leaving behind the capelin, the whale headed back to the surface and slapped his tail off the surface, warning the would-be predator of its massive size. The humpback whale dove back down but could still sense the predator circling below, each rotation getting closer as it prepared to make its move. The whale sped towards the surface and breached, the entire thirty tonnes exploding through the surface waters as it jumped clear out of the water. It made an enormous splash upon re-entry, sending a thunderous boom echoing throughout the ocean. For now, whatever lurked in the shadows had disappeared.

Atlantic Ocean
Cliffs of the Grand Banks

Joan felt the shock wave as the humpback whale crashed back into the ocean, and dove back down to four-hundred metres. The whale would be more than enough to sustain her and the pack of male Carcharodons following her trail of hormones. She kept far enough away so that the humpback couldn't sense her, biding her time before she made her strike. She needed to disable the mighty whale's tail. One smack from its powerful tail would be devastating, even to a shark of her size. For now, she cruised along, her jaws slightly open in a mean snarl as she waited for an opening. She would be able to wound the whale if she managed to catch the bull off guard.

Joan sensed the smaller great whites closing in on her, sensing she was growing tired and weak from the chase. It had been days since her last significant meal. The odd creature that she found swimming in the waters wasn't big enough to sustain her for long. Her stomach was growling with pain as the muscles tightened from starvation. Her body had undergone a lot of changes since reaching sexual maturity. Her calorie intake had doubled to get ready for bearing pups. Joan continued along the drop off of the Grand Banks as the whale chased a school of smaller fish closer to shore. She wasn't going to be able to attack in these shallow waters. There wouldn't be enough room for her to escape if her attack failed. Her body was growing impatient with her, waiting for its opportunity to feed.

CCGS **Cape Spear**
Atlantic Ocean
Grand Banks

Kevin used his GPS to guide the CCGS *Cape Spear* towards the last sighting of a humpback whale the fisherman reported seeing near Cape Race. They estimated the giant whale to be well over fifty feet. The local news crew paid handsomely to hitch a ride with the Canadian Coast Guard. Lewis stayed behind on the docks, waiting to meet some marine biologist. Kevin was glad to have command of the ship without Lewis bothering him. Melvin poked his head into the cabin occasionally to preach to him about one thing then the other, but, like most of his crew, Melvin stuck around with the locally famous weatherman. What made things even worse was that his wife wasn't talking to him, making him sleep on the couch. His back

ached from the old wooden beam that ran down the cen-
tre of the couch. He didn't get much sleep last night after
a long fight about nothing. She thought he was cheating
on her with some floozy he met at some bar; she didn't
believe him when he said he was spending long hours trying to work on the McGilvery case. It was out of charac-
ter for him and beyond his job description, but Labyrinth
Oil paid him and Lewis a substantial amount of money
to help keep things out of the media. Specifically, they
didn't want the media to find out about the giant squid's
tooth they had found. Mr. Kurosawa said it would give
the activists a reason to shut down the pipeline. Since the
Architeuthis dux was an endangered species, the pipeline
would be shut down instantly if they decided to take up
residence along the its path.

The camera man stood alongside the rail, taking footage of the large swells as the weatherman tried to explain
how global warming was creating the large waves. He also
predicted another foggy day because of the cold Labrador
Current and the intense heat of the sun. Kevin had heard
it all before, and he still wasn't buying in to the scientific
concepts related to global warming. To him it just wasn't
plausible. The way some people talked about the phenomenon, it would be the end of the world, an apocalypse
to end all of humanity. The earth always found a way of
balancing itself out. The melting ice caps and rising ocean
levels would be balanced out later by something else, all
part of the plan.

The nose of the ship cut through a four-foot swell,
sending a spray of ocean mist over local weather man Edward Sheaves. Kevin laughed as the stalky man reacted

like someone had slapped him in the face, terrified by some unexplained force. The saline water dripped down from his balding hair and over his microphone as he hunched over to shield himself from another blow. Kevin glanced at the ship's navigational system and found it hard to believe he was only twenty nautical miles from his destination. The fog rolling in over the waves made it appear like they were segregated from the land, trapped out in the middle of the ocean, isolated on all sides by nothing but blue water and groggy looking clouds. The ocean floor was just one hundred metres below. He hadn't even arrived at the drop off of the Grand Banks yet.

Melvin walked into the cabin; salt water soaked into his jacket, leaving behind white stains on the sleek black fabric as the heat baked it. "Hey, Kevin, Edward Sheaves wanted to do an interview with you about discovering the *Swift Current*."

"Did you tell him that Lewis is taking the lead on this one?" Kevin didn't want to be publicly involved, but it would help smooth things over with his wife if he was on news. It would give his story credibility.

"I didn't think that mattered," Melvin grumbled. "So, what do you want me to tell him?"

"It's fine, Melvin. I'll do it," Kevin called out, not wanting to miss his opportunity to prove to his wife he wasn't lying about working the McGilvery case. "Just give me some time to get my thoughts together." He didn't want to say too much. The police investigation was gathering intel as it heated up. They were closing in on two local fisherman that had motives and no alibi other than each other, and their story didn't seem to add up.

"Thanks, Kevin." Melvin softened his tone. "I'm proud of you for letting Lewis take the lead on this case." It had been Melvin's idea to let Lewis take control over the search for Jonah McGilvery. So far it had been working in Kevin's favor.

"Just let me get us to the humpback whale. Maybe they can get some footage of the whale during my interview. I know that would draw the ratings on the evening broadcast."

Atlantic Ocean
Cliffs of the Grand Banks

The bull whale thrashed its tail on the surface of the water, trapping the capelin in a net of bubbles. The small fish were caught in the shrinking ring, unable to find a way out of the closing trap. The mighty humpback whale opened his garage-door-sized mouth, the fish caught in the flow of water entering its stomach as it swam into the school of capelin. Thousands of the tiny fish disappeared down its throat to be digested in its giant stomach. When the bull's stomach was filled with fish and water, he swam to the surface to squeeze the excess water out through the baleen plates in his mouth. Finally feeling sated, the giant whale allowed half of his brain to rest, the other half taking control of his base instincts. The whale would drift with the tidal currents underneath the choppy surface waves. When he needed oxygen the mammal's primal instincts would take over and propel him to the surface to get the air he needed.

Atlantic Ocean
Cliffs of the Grand Banks

Joan could sense the lumbering giant drifting aim-lessly through the waters. The electrical impulses from the enormous muscles had all but stopped. The whale's heartbeat had slowed to nearly a stop as he floated just below the surface. Joan rose from the depths quickly, clos-ing the gap to one hundred metres. She circled directly below the creature, waiting for the electrical impulses from his giant heart to quicken, but her prey still didn't feel her presence. Joan dove straight down so she would be able to generate enough force to seriously injure the whale with one quick strike. At two-hundred metres the *Carcharodon carcharias* rushed the whale, his giant shadow blotting out much of the sunlight from the surface. The massive silhouette didn't move until it was too late. The great white shark slammed hard into the whale's under-belly, her razor-sharp teeth grasping on to a large jaw-ful of blubber. Joan thrashed her body from side to side. With her jaws clamped shut, she tore a hunk of meat off. A flood of warm blood washed over her as she extended her jaws to bite into the severed whale flesh. She sensed the whale's tail muscles exploding to life; she dove just in time to avoid the swift defensive blow from the giant appendage.

A flood of deep red blood poured into the ocean from the bull whale's wound. It wasn't dead, but it was severe-ly wounded. The whale cried out in pain, bemoaning the effort it took to stay on the surface as it bled to death. The whale was far too strong for Joan to mount another at-tack. The piece of blubber she swallowed would have to

be enough for now. She waited patiently for the humpback's electrical impulses to fade away before she would
strike again. The scent of blood filled the ocean. The male
white sharks that had been chasing Joan quickly closed in,
no longer keeping their distance. With the strong scent of
blood mixing with her estrus, the aroma drove them into
a frenzy, making them brave. They took turns rushing the
giant humpback, not getting close enough for a taste but
close enough to make the bull defend himself. The dying
whale had to spend a great deal of energy thrashing its
tail in self-defence, causing its heart to pump harder. Gal-
lons of blood spewed from the gnarly gash on its stomach.
The whale struggled to keep its body right side up. His
massive thirty-tonne frame rolled over, exposing the creature to a barrage of savage attacks from the snapping jaws
filled with rows upon rows of teeth.

Joan sensed the last flicker from the creature's heart,
ascending towards the carcass to fill her gullet with
enough whale blubber to last her for days. An overpower-
ing bouquet of impulses had sent the sharks into a frenzy
as a giant pool of blood washed over them. Joan was just
about to snap her jaws closed on the exposed stomach of
the whale when one of the males took her by surprise,
ramming his jaws into her gills to get a better grasp on
her. Joan tried to fight the male shark off, but he held on
long enough to commit the brutal ritual of mating. Once
it was all over, Joan was exhausted from the ordeal and
needed to feed. She made her way back to the whale carcass to eat.

CCGS **Cape Spear**
Atlantic Ocean
Humpback Whale Carcass

A giant blood stain floated around the humpback whale as he bobbed up and down in the water. Kevin could smell the coppery scent of blood and the potent tinge of ammonia that flooded out of the creature and into the ocean waters. Edward Sheaves plugged his nose as he buckled over at the hips, clutching his belly as he suppressed the urge to vomit. "Jesus Christ, what the hell happened here." Kevin looked over at Melvin.

Melvin was using the binoculars to get a better look at the floating cadaver. "It looks like something tore it up," Melvin muttered to himself as he peered through the lenses. "Not that long ago that somebody reported seeing the whale here in the harbour. It was only three, four hours."

Kevin checked his watch. "Looking at just over three hours. Do you think it ran into the boat's outboard motor?"

"Not possible. We would have gotten a report from the vessel that collided with a beast this size." Melvin shook his head in disbelief. "Whatever did this is still down there somewhere."

"What the hell could have attacked a bull that size?" Kevin asked. "It could capsize this boat with a flick of its tail if it had the notion." Kevin slowed the engine down, not wanting to get too close to the dead whale's corpse. The image of a squid tentacle rising from the depths and clutching hold of his ship raced through his mind. Imaging a giant mouth filled with filed teeth opening wide as the tentacles dragged people into its mouth made Kevin's heart beat a little faster.

Edward flew to the rail and let the contents of his stomach drop overboard into the ocean. He leaned into the metal pole, a strand of vomit dangling from his lips as the breeze picked up. "You didn't get that on film, did you?" He looked over his shoulder with a defeated expression on his face.

"No, boss." The cameraman looked over at Kevin and winked, giving him a thumbs up. The red light on the video camera was blinking.

Melvin held up his finger to his face, trying to hush everyone on board. Kevin stopped to listen, all he could hear was the sound of the waves crashing against the shore and the weatherman heaving up his guts. "What is it, Melvin?" Kevin asked puzzled.

"Listen carefully. I can hear something tearing at the whale carcass." Melvin closed his eyes to enhance his hearing ability. The *Cape Spear* drifted towards the humpback whale slowly now, the boat entering the blood slick. "I can almost feel it."

Edward Sheaves suddenly jumped back from the rail and tripped up in his own feet, dragging himself backwards towards the middle of the ship. A horrified expression was plastered on his pale face. His jaw dropped open with astonishment. The cameraman kept the video rolling, getting his boss on film. It would probably never make it on air, but it would definitely be shown to his friends. A giant grin appeared on his face as he watched Edward shiver with fear.

"Sh… Sh… Shark," Edward stammered.

Kevin approached the railing to get a better look

overboard. The water was thick with blood and guts, the whale's entrails floating on the surface. Something was churning up the water just below the belly of the giant humpback. Bubbles of air churned up through the bloodied mess making it hard to see. Then a grey dorsal fin created a ripple as it approached the whale. A dorsal fin kept rising from the water, standing nearly three-feet tall when the back of the shark finally emerged from the water. The shark's jaw snapped open and shut in an instant, tearing into a hunk of whale blubber. The shark's caudal fin thrashed from violently side to side as it shook its head, stripping the flesh from the humpback whale. When it finally tore off a piece big enough, it dove below the water. Another set of jaws clasped onto the whale to get its share of the food.

"What the hell is going on, Melvin?" Kevin had never seen anything like this before in his life. "Those sharks are massive." Every shark had to be at least twenty feet. Tall dorsal fins emerged from below everywhere as the sharks devoured the massive humpback whale in a frenzied state.

Melvin didn't wait for Kevin. He went into the cabin and put the boat in reverse. Some sharks were over half the length of the forty-foot search and rescue ship. Kevin grabbed Edward by the collar of his shirt and dragged him into the cabin without protest.

"Thank you," Edward said as he clutched the cabin wall.

"Get in here!" Melvin called to the cameraman who had moved closer to the rails to get a better shot. The boat sank into the swells and rose up on the crest of the waves, a bloodied sea splashing up over the decking of the ship. The cameraman held his video camera in one hand and braced himself against the rail with the other. "Hey, asshole, get in here before a wave tosses ya overboard!" Melvin barked.

"Come on, Sam, get in here. We got enough footage now." Edward's tone was full of dread for his daredevil friend, but he refused to leave the security of the cabin.

Kevin headed back outside. The clouds parted overhead, and the sun lit up the gruesome scene with visceral visuals. A giant puddle formed around the massacre. Bloodied water was saturated with scrapes of whale skin and guts, and tiny shreds of intestines floated in the water. The humpback whale's flesh was torn to pieces. No more blood flowed from the mammal's wound, but the body still shook as sharks pulled and tugged at the remaining blubber. "Come on, Sam…" Kevin started to say as one of the sharks slammed its tail fin into the boat, the vibrations rocking the entire hull of the *Cape Spear*. "Sam, get back in the cabin!" Kevin growled as he reached out just in time to catch Sam. A rogue wave crashed over the side of the ship, nearly sweeping Sam off his feet. He let the camera drop to his side as Kevin pulled him away from the railing. "That was too fucking close," Kevin said.

Melvin steered the boat in the opposite direction of the feeding frenzy and pushed the engines to capacity, leaving the grisly scene behind them. "Were those great whites?" Edward asked, his body still trembling with fear.

"I think so. What other species of shark gets that large?" Sam questioned.

"No one has ever reported white sharks in these waters." Kevin was still processing what he had just seen. "There must have been a dozen of them."

"I got some excellent footage." Sam sounded jovial.

"Too gruesome to air on the news, Sam," Edward added. "We won't be able to show that."

"I can edit the footage. We have to let people know what happened here," Sam protested.

"Melvin, how far away is the Labyrinth Oil pipeline?" Kevin remembered the divers started their work today. The blood in that water would attract all the sharks around for miles, putting them in a frenzied state.

"I'd say bout ten miles, maybe less." Melvin picked up the radio receiver. "Dispatch come in."

CHAPTER FOURTEEN

Labyrinth Oil Office
St. John's, Newfoundland

Kal Kurosawa looked down onto the street from his office window, shaking his head at the protesters. The crowd around the building slowly formed into a mob. First the fishermen gathered to protest the closure of the ports all over the southern coast, then the animal rights activists showed up to protect the migrating whales. Now a group of environmentalists led by Madeline Northcott joined in the protest to fight against the company. He observed as she rallied her troops. Madeline's fist pumped in the air as her fellow hipster friends lifted up their arms at whatever nonsense she was spewing against Labyrinth Oil.

"A message for you, Mr. Kurosawa," his secretary buzzed in through the speaker on his computer.

"What is it now?" Kal found himself growing frustrated with everything. The moment Jonah had gone missing, all the responsibilities had been thrust onto his lap. He didn't have time to deal with Jonah's obligations, he had his own agenda to carry out.

"It's from the Canadian Coast Guard. They say there is a pack of sharks close to the pipeline."

"Thanks. I'll deal with it." Kal didn't take his eyes off the growing mob. Their angry protesting rose above the sounds of traffic from twenty stories down, and the boisterous noise was growing louder. Jonah McGilvery hired Kal to handle one unique aspect of the organization. The analysts discovered something much more valuable than oil beneath the Grand Banks. A complex network of underground caverns underneath the pocket of oil contained something precious and unique. There was enough plutonium and uranium in these grottoes to sustain the world with clean energy for generations to come. The plutonium could also be used to power nuclear weapons. Jonah had always told him it wasn't up to him what the end-user did with the radioactive element. It was Kal's job to find the highest bidder. So far the United States government was hell bent on being just that, offering to add ten percent to the highest bid. Kal had the president of the United States bowing to his every command, applying the leverage from other offers to blackmail the entire country.

Kal couldn't afford to suspend production of the pipeline. He sat at his desk to make a phone call. If there were threats swimming around his workers they needed to be eliminated. He dialed the top-secret number that went straight to the oval office. The sharks would be dealt with one way or another. There wasn't a chance he would halt production now when they were so close to the caverns. For now, he needed to create a distraction that would draw people's attention away from the pipeline. Kal had to convince the police to arrest a suspect in the Jonah

McGilvery case. That should draw the media's attention back towards the land and away from his operation. Kal headed into the elevator and put in his key that would grant him access to Jonah's private suite. He would plant evidence in some poor man's boat and pay off one cop to find it. He came up with a diabolical plot to kill two birds with one stone. That chirping birdie outside needed to be silenced long enough to finish this project.

Grand Banks
Atlantic Ocean

The *Carcharodon carcharias* could sense a vast array of signals, distinguishing small foreign objects that entered its domain. Joan could sense the exact moment when a ship dropped anchor, the reverberations alerting her lateral line of the slightest tremors even from immeasurable distances. Joan had learned that these objects were inedible. Normally she didn't bother to investigate, but she could sense the fluttering heartbeat of several creatures near these large sections of foreign metal in the ocean. She wasn't the only great white who took notice; a ferocious pack swam towards the mile-long pipeline being laid by Labyrinth Oil and the unsuspecting workers.

Labyrinth Oil Pipeline
Grand Banks
Atlantic Ocean

The turbulent seas slowed the progress of the pipeline. Darren Pike fought with the controls to keep his one-man submarine steady, the active currents knocking the sub around like a play toy when he didn't exercise caution. Divers welded the giant sections of titanium pipe together from the inside first. The opening of the pipeline spanned nearly ten feet in diameter with pumps at every junction to flush out the sea water once the pipe was finished being put together. One-hundred metre sections of pipeline weighed several tonnes and weren't affected by the current. Driving the sub proved to be treacherous, and entering the entrance of the pipe as the ocean current surged inside was problematic. Bright white lights from his underwater submersible illuminated the darkest depths of the ocean floor, sending the aquatic life scattering for shade. The odd fish would swim past occasionally curious about the subs, but nothing caused them any anxiety. Jagged rocks covering the sea floor were covered in dense algae and rusted out old metal parts. Seaweed drifted in the current, waving in the water as if blowing in the breeze. Beyond the reach of the bright lights all Darren saw was a blanket of darkness. Fish would appear out of nowhere as if by some magic trick as they drifted through the work zone and disappeared again into thin air.

Several of the workers had injured themselves as the strong current smashed them into the outer edge of the giant cylinders. Mr. Kurosawa insisted that production of the pipeline not be delayed. Several of the workers found themselves forced to work double shifts, not getting enough time in between dives. They had quickly depleted their workforce but were awaiting the arrival of another five hundred workers. The problem wasn't finding the laborers; transporting them from the airport to the work site unnoticed proved challenging. Mobs of angry fisherman begged for the work, but Mr. Kurosawa had insisted that the jobs be supplied by an American corporation.

Darren had worked on Labyrinth Oil's first pipeline, but something bizarre was going on here. When Mr. McGilvery built the original pipeline, safety first had been their motto. Now the demand to finish the task on time overruled all, the schedule rigid and strict. Mr. Kurosawa would not tolerate failure as an option. Darren had not seen a price too high to pay to get the job done. Several of the workers suffered severe injuries just to have another person take their place to do the same job. One poor soul had broken his back as the current slammed him hard into the titanium edge of the pipeline. Darren was one of the lucky few who got to control the one-man submersibles.

The Sea Welder Model Five or SW-5 was designed and modified from the older army model by Labyrinth Oil. Scientists at Labyrinth Oil originally designed the sub to make quick repairs to damaged war vessels when they found it impossible to make it back to port. They had modified the new design with four sets of arms, each with a unique ability to work underwater. One pair of arms could be used to pick up large sheets of metal. Another set functioned to weld the sections of pipe together, and a third set was used to cut them apart. The final set was designed to make precise movements that could be used for a wide variety of tasks normally saved for the divers. Darren's skills allowed him to use the arms to tie a knot in a rope if he wanted too. The whole cockpit of the sub was clear, made from a three-inch Plexiglas windshield able to withstand pressures found at depths up to 1,000 metres. The view was only obstructed by the flashing lights on his control panel, the bright LED lights reflecting off the clear glass.

Darren waited for one of the divers to give him the signal to weld the next section of pipeline together so the workers inside could move on. Paranoia crept over him, the vast depths of the ocean playing tricks on his mind as he stared off into the bleak surroundings. It had been about twenty minutes since the welders had made their way inside, but it seemed like an eternity to Darren. The pressures of the deep waters pushed down hard on the SW-5's hull, causing her to creak and groan in the eerie silence. At only 400 metres down the pressure was reaching dangerously high levels. Management should cut the divers' shifts in half, but Mr. Kurosawa insisted they stay down much longer until the next crew arrived. It was only a matter of time before there was another serious accident.

A pyramid snout poked through the dark veil and entered the light. Darren froze as the snarled, tooth-filled smile emerged from the darkness. Cold, black eyes peered at him as it turned its head back and forth taking in its surroundings. The shark's entire body drifted into view gradually, its grey body emerging from the darkness inch by inch. With minimum effort, the great white shark moved its tail fin gliding from side to side. Propelling the colossal frame through the deep waters with ease, it moved gracefully. Its two large nares guided the shark towards the opening of the pipe. Darren tensed up. His heart froze in his chest as he watched the white shark swim towards the crew trapped inside. For a moment, time seemed to stand still as Darren watched hopelessly. Instinct told him to turn and run. His blood ran cold and his body perspired profusely.

He snapped to his senses, realizing that he was operating a submersible, not swimming with the shark. He grabbed the controls of the SW-5 and pushed the throttle forward in an attempt to deter the *Carcharodon carcharias*. Momentarily forgetting the arms were still connected to the titanium pipe, his submersible banked at a sharp angle nearly causing a collision with the pipe. Darren flicked the release switch just before he ran out of space, sending the SW-5 into a tight barrel roll to avoid crashing. Turning back towards the opening to the pipeline, Darren saw nothing. The lights illuminated the sea floor but nothing else. Had he hallucinated the whole encounter with the shark? He had heard of other divers suffering from deep sea psychosis. Some people had called it the rapture of the deep, and others called it aberrations of the deep, but it was all caused by the same thing. Ambient pressure from the ocean mixed nitrogen into the divers' lungs causing nitrogen narcosis, a dangerous problem which could lead to these symptoms and worse: an unconsciousness which was often fatal at these depths.

Darren maneuvered his submersible towards the mouth of the pipeline, the bright lights illuminating the gates of hell. He rubbed his eyes and pinched himself but the demonic setting didn't disappear. Divers tried to swim past the massive shark as its jaws snapped shut on a man's leg. In a rapid motion, thrashing its head side to side, the shark tore the man's leg clean off, releasing a gush of crimson inside the enclosure. As people swam through the horrific blood-filled pipe, they immediately swam straight towards the surface in a desperate attempt to escape the shark's wrath. The blood had attracted more great whites, the scent of blood guiding them to the helpless swimmers. A shark set its sights on Darren, swimming straight into the Plexiglas of his sub. The powerful smack sent Darren spinning through the water. A thin crack formed in the protective glass. Darren held his breath as the water pressure slowly pried open the crack. At first a trickle of water poured into the cockpit before giving way to a flood of salty ocean water. Darren pushed the throttle fully forward and raced towards the surface. His lungs burned as the light of the sun seemed so distant. The surface seemed much further away as he struggled to keep conscious. Darren saw the white caps on the waves of the surface just before he blacked out. The sub broke the rough surface just moments after sea water filled his lungs.

Labyrinth Oil Office
St. John's, Newfoundland

"I understand. Make certain that no one finds out about what took place. I will handle the rest. You just keep this out of the news." Mr. Kurosawa slammed the phone down, nearly knocking the receiver off the table. The next crew wouldn't be ready to dive for another six hours, and now he would need an entirely new team to be flown in. Thanks to Jonah's death, he was already two days behind schedule, and he had already spent over half of the money given to Labyrinth Oil by the American government. Pressure from foreign sources increased. Building this massive pipeline had cost a fortune already, and now he would have to ask for another advance. He dreaded the thought of dishing out capital to the families of the deceased just to keep them silent.

The elevator door opened with a metallic swooshing sound. Miss Eguchi stepped out wearing a black dress with a wide silver ribbon around the midriff. The dress fell just below her knees but a long slit up the side revealed her toned thigh muscle. Her red high-heeled shoes clicked off the floor as she walked towards him. She was caring a beige file folder under her arm which she placed on the table, leaning her hands on the top of the folder as she leaned in towards Kal.

"What's all of this?" Kal asked, trying to avoid staring down her dress.

She opened the folder, spreading the sheets out over his desk. "It's a list of all the family members we need to silence." She held up one page. The worker's name was listed on top and below was his family members and contact info. "This is going to cost us millions of dollars."

"Don't you think I realize that, Hilary?" Kal raised his voice in frustration. "We can't stop now."

Hilary put the papers back into the folder and closed it. "What do we do if people aren't willing to take the offer?"

"We do the same thing we had to do the last time we had this problem." Kal pushed the folder away. "Do you need the number or do you still have it?"

"I still have it, but I won't be responsible for taking any more lives." Miss Eguchi snatched up the folder. "If you want it done, you can call yourself."

Kal avoided Hilary's scornful glare. "Just give me a list of the names of people unwilling to cooperate and I will take care of it." Hilary stormed out of his office; her slate-blue eyes welled with tears. It worried him, what his brother would say if he ever found out about what he made his wife do. He had forced her to do horrible things for him since the first day they worked together. Over the past five years she had grown to loath him, but he threatened to kill her husband if she ever told him what they really did. The lies, deception, and cruel actions would bring shame upon their family.

Kal picked up the remote and turned on the sixty-inch high-definition television. The local news was just starting. The anchor was announcing the day's top stories for tonight's program. Kal's blood pressure started to rise as he saw the footage of great white sharks tearing into a deceased whale carcass. He threw the remote clear across the room as a clip of the reporter was getting ready to interview Kevin O'Reilly showed. "I don't have time for this." He was about to retrieve the remote and change the channel when he read the headline. *Labyrinth Oil to blame for the sudden presence of great white sharks.* Kal's blood pressure soared. Turning up the volume he listened as Kevin blamed his company for the sudden appearance of great white sharks in the coastal waters of Newfoundland. *"Since they started laying the titanium pipe they've been showing up. They must be attracted to the metal they're using to build their new oil pipeline."* Kal slammed his fist against the table in a fit of rage.

Kal opened his desk drawer and took out a locked box as he cursed under his breath. Using the key, he opened the safe and dialed the number written on the lone piece of paper that had been kept secure inside. He needed to silence Kevin O'Reilly before he attracted more attention to Labyrinth Oil's latest project. Not only would the investigation hold up the pipeline, it could potentially squash any deal they had made with the American government.

"I need another favor and I require it done now. Money won't be an issue."

CHAPTER FIFTEEN

The Marine Institute
St. John's, NL

The cab driver spoke the whole fifteen-minute cab drive from the airport to the Marine Institute, no matter how hard Andy tried to avoid carrying on the conversation. Andy had been trying to gather his thoughts after that rough landing. His nerves were rattled. The grey-haired taxi driver spoke quickly, many of his words blending into the others, making it difficult to follow what he was saying. His accent was heavy, and his voice was hoarse which didn't help matters. The backseat smelled like cigarette smoke and vomit from the night before. "Uhm.... How much do I owe you?" Andy asked.

"Dats gonna be eighty-four dollars." The cab driver leaned his head into the back of the car. His haggard smile was filled with yellow teeth.

Andy pulled out his wallet and handed him five of the twenty-dollar bills that Ellen had given him before they left the airport. "Keep the change." Andy didn't wait for a response. He threw open the door and dragged his suit-case right behind him as the taxi driver yelled out something. The sun was hiding behind the clouds, but its presence was felt. The air was hot and muggy. Andy couldn't wait to check into a hotel and get a shower. He could feel his shirt clinging to his damp armpits. He headed down a paved path towards the giant glass entrance to the building. Above the doors, in giant white lettering, the name of the building was displayed *The Marine Institute of St. John's University of Newfoundland*. The glass looked deep blue, mimicking the deep ocean waters. The large double doors opened into a giant reception hall. Rows of large white pillars and the marbled floor made it look like the lost city of Atlantis from the books he used to read as a child.

"Good day, sir. Can I help you?" a young woman sat behind the wicket asked gently.

"I'm here to see Doctor Hamilton."

"You must be Doctor Grant." The woman sprang to her feet and came out from her tiny office to great him. Her maroon tee shirt was embroidered with the university's logo in white letters. Her short blond hair was gelled into several sharp looking spikes that must have taken hours to get just right. Her white rimmed glasses made her look like the typical university hipster from some teen movie. "It's so great you could make it."

Andy reached out to shake her hand and was surprised by the girl's powerful grip, the knuckles on his hand cracking as she applied pressure. "Call me, Andy. And who might you be?"

"My name is Samantha, but my friends call me Sami." She blushed as she smiled at him.

"Nice to meet you, Sami." Andy looked around the

room at the various plaques and statues strategically placed around the room. "So, should I wait here for Doctor Hamilton?"

"Don't be silly. I'll take you down right now if you'd like." Sami's emerald eyes looked longingly at Andy.

"Sure, that would be fine."

Sami turned right and started to point to the statues as they headed down a long hallway. "These are all the past deans of the university," she explained as she began to lead him towards a set of double doors. "This part of the university nearly closed a few years ago until we opened it up to the public. Now it is one of the most popular attractions on the east coast of Newfoundland. Which is great considering how important the ocean is to our existence." Sami nearly talked as fast as the taxi driver, but at least he could pick out all the separate words. "Doctor Hamilton's work has been featured in several scientific magazines. I'm sure you must have heard of her. Her thesis on the effects of the melting ice caps on the waters off the Grand Banks has been ground breaking." Sami continued to gush.

Andy chuckled a little. "I haven't heard her name before, but to be honest I don't read many of those magazines anymore." Andy was ashamed to admit it, but over the last few years he only focused on sharks so he'd look better on television. He devoted his life solely to learning all he could about the *Carcharodon carcharias* and hadn't taken the time to broaden his horizons. "Caught up in my own studies." There was an awkward silence for a moment, only their footsteps echoed down the hallway. Andy wasn't sure if the girl was being polite or shocked by his revelation, but now he wished he had just agreed with her. "This place is kinda quiet today huh?" They passed by empty classrooms and laboratories.

"A lot of our students are out on the water learning how take samples, and some are gone on a whale watching expedition," Sami said as they passed by the cafeteria. The smell of deep-fried foods made Andy's mouth water. "So, tell me what brings you to Newfoundland?"

"Well, actually, we have tracked a *Carcharodon carcharias* all the way from South Africa to here." Andy didn't want to mention anything about his theory of the sharks' mating ground. "Her satellite tag sent several signals from the southern coast of the island."

"That's so cool." Sami's voice was filled with awe. They turned a corner and a crowd of people were walking around admiring some sea life through the display tanks. "The exhibit is busy today. I guess word got out that a great white was brought here." Children pressed their faces to the tank making faces at the codfish as they swam by, ignoring the do not tap on the glass sign hung from the corner on a white sign.

"So, this keeps the university running, very clever," Andy said as he watched a little boy chase after another, running in and out of the displays as their mother buried her nose in her cell phone.

"Darnold could you at least try to enforce the safety rules," Sami yelled out to a gawky teen across the room. The young man looked up from the floor but couldn't see the problem, his glasses nearly sliding off his greasy face as he looked up. "No running, kids." The children didn't listen. Their mother, her face cast in the dull white glow of her phone, called out to them half-heartedly.

"So, you guys put the great white on display some-where?" Andy looked around at all the tanks, trying to spot his fish.

Sami shook her head. "No, we kept the shark out back. Only staff are allowed out there. It's right this way if you'll follow me." Sami led Andy through a door at the back of the room and into a working cell of scientific holding tanks. The frigid cold of the ocean wrapped itself around Andy as two giant filtration systems pumped cold salt water through the pipes overhead. A young woman wearing a white lab coat was bent over the shark's carcass, kneeling down on one knee as she took a photograph. The light from the camera illuminated the pure white belly of the *Carcharodon* pup. The open jaw revealed the still de-veloping teeth which were still an inch long just months after birth. Ellen's film crew was gathered around the sev-en-foot body of the shark, getting all of their equipment ready for Andy. Their cab must have arrived long before his, giving them a chance to set up.

"Doctor Hamilton, your guest is here."

The young woman was startled by Sami's voice, nearly leaping out of her black rubber boots. She turned around quickly as she regained her balance. Her cheeks were rosy red from the cold, and her eyes had such a light shade of blue they were almost grey. Her chestnut brown hair was tied into a messy knot atop her head, the light shimmering in the glossy hair spray she used to keep it under control. "You must be Doctor Grant." A jubilant smile crossed her face. She held the camera tightly to her chest.

"Nice to meet you, Doctor Hamilton." Andy extended his hand, but Kate ignored the gesture, staring at him like a school girl. "Please call me Andy."

"You can call me Kate." Her voice was high pitched. "I'm so glad you could make it here so fast."

"I was actually on the way here for research anyway. I see you met my crew." Andy waved to them. They nodded at him as they set up the camera.

"Ready when you are, Andy."

"So, you obviously didn't need me to identify the shark. This is a perfect specimen." Andy admired the great white shark's textbook perfect signs. The pure white belly, even the dark grey back side had no signs of scarring or indication of disease. The pectoral fins were nearly a foot long, its dorsal fin in perfect condition. "So how can I help you?" he asked.

"Well it's the cause of death." Kate pointed to the shark's belly.

"No signs of disease." Andy bent down and looked at the grey organs in its belly. "Have you opened her stomach lining? I've seen great whites try to eat things that are too big and block their throats off. They basically starve to death as they can't pass food down to their digestive track."

"I didn't open anything. I didn't want to touch anything." Kate kept looking at the camera as she spoke.

"Ignore the camera, just pretend it's you and me here." Andy motioned for the cameraman to push back slightly. "It looks silly on television." Andy looked around the shark's insides. "Are you sure nothing fell out when you cut him open?"

"I didn't cut him open." Kate defended herself. "This is how the shark was brought in to us."

Andy pushed his hand inside the slime-covered opening, pushing the organs around inside. "The shark's liver is missing. Do you know if there are any orcas around the area the shark was found?"

Kate picked up a clipboard and flipped through some pages. "The captain that brought the body in said that the killer whales seemed to be playing with the shark. Tossing it up into the air."

"Killer whales have been known to feed on the nutrient-rich livers of great white sharks. We still don't know how they are able to do it, but they can remove the liver with as much precision as a surgeon." Andy used his television voice for the camera, hoping to generate a great sound clip for the show. "I haven't heard of many great white sharks being discovered off the coast of Newfoundland. Do you get many?"

Kate shook her head and scrunched up her nose. "It's extraordinarily rare to discover them so close. I don't think we've ever encountered one so young."

"We certainly have stumbled across something here." Andy used his most mysterious voice, hamming it up for the camera.

"Cut."

"So how do you think the shark ended up in our waters? How old do you think it is?" Kate asked once the camera stopped rolling.

"Hey, guys, can we get the camera rolling again. This will be great for the show." Andy waited for the cameraman to hoist the heavy piece of equipment back onto his shoulder. "Kate, can you ask that same question again please."

Kate looked at the camera, dumbfounded. "So old do you think the shark is?"

"No, the other question, please." Andy was ready to divulge his theory. "We can edit this later right?" The cameraman shot Andy a thumbs up from behind the large piece of equipment.

"How do you think the shark appeared in Newfound-land?" Kate seemed uncomfortable in front of the camera now, her eyebrows furled.

"Well, Doctor Hamilton, I believe the pup was birthed here," Andy started to explain. "I have a theory that the *Carcharodon carcharias* are brought back to these cold Atlantic waters by instinct. They travel thousands of miles to mate and give birth near the Grand Banks. The nutrient-rich water is filled with abundant sources of food, and their natural predators are very rare in these waters." Andy stared straight at the camera. "It's the ideal nursery for a young generation to grow up and learn how to survive before migrating to other oceans."

"Cut," the cameraman said without much enthusiasm.

"Thanks for everything, Kate." Andy smiled wide, showing his bright white teeth. He felt like the interview went great, and it would make an interesting part of the documentary if his theory planned out.

"You don't actually accept that a great white shark gave birth to that pup here do you?" Kate questioned him. "I mean, that species of shark is not prevalent in these waters?"

"I actually do, and I have facts that back up my theory that the great white shark is perfectly capable of keeping itself hidden from humans if they choose." Andy defended his thesis.

Kate looked down at the shark carcass. "Wouldn't we have seen signs of them? Dead whales should have been more common than they are." Kate shook her head in disagreement.

"Maybe they have been eating other sources of food." Andy wasn't giving an inch. He was growing more confident with every clue. "We just have to find what they've been feeding on and I'll find them."

Kate stood in silence for a moment. "Do great whites eat squid?"

"Great whites will eat just about anything, but there would have to be a lot of cuttlefish in these waters to sustain their appetites." Andy knew that it was possible but highly improbable.

"What about a giant *Arcitheuthis dux*?"

Andy nodded his head in agreement. "That should do the trick. Thanks for the advice, I know that's going to help me find that shark nursery." Andy turned to leave but stopped when Kate's hand reached out and clutched his shoulder. He turned back towards her, her slate-blue eyes staring intently back at him.

"I'm coming with you."

CCGS **Heart's Content**
St. John's Harbour

"How much is this costing us?" Ellen complained as she carried her suitcase aboard the Canadian Coast Guard ship. The wheels got stuck on the rungs as she dragged it up the ramp, the bottom of the metal plank clanking off the wooden wharf as the waves rocked the boat side to side.

"Nowhere near as much as some of those private ships," Derrick answered as he carried a heavy metal briefcase in each hand. The satellite tracking equipment was heavy. The amplifiers needed to track the signal in the open sea weighed over fifty pounds each.

"It will all be worth it when we find Joan." Andy rubbed his fingers against his thumb, gesturing the universal sign for money with his free hand. "Besides, this is probably the only ship that can house all of us. I think we will be out here for a few days until we finally find her."

"And why is she here again?" Ellen stared back at the wharf as Kate Hamilton spoke with the young captain of the vessel. Her maroon university sweater made her look more like a freshman than a professor. "I'm not paying her for this."

"Don't worry about it, she's glad to come along as long as I agree to let the university capitalize on the newfound discovery of a shark nursery in their own backyard." Andy looked up as Ellen disappeared behind the gunwale of the ship, the rails obscuring her from his view. "Besides, I need her to help track down the giant *Arcitheuthis dux* in order to find out where the whites have been hiding all these years!" Andy yelled out.

"I thought you had a signal from your shark?" Ellen looked over the railing and down at Andy.

"She pinged on our system not two hours ago, but if she doesn't surface for another few days, then the tag become useless," Derrick piped up.

Andy reached the deck of the *CCGS Heart's Content*

and was caught off guard by how luxurious the search and rescue ship was. The forty-eight foot long and eighteen-foot wide vessel was brand new, the crown jewel for the Atlantic's search and rescue fleet. The paint still hadn't faded from the salt sea mists. There wasn't a sign of rust anywhere on the sleek deck. There were four levels below deck on the ship. The bottom level housed all the mechanical rooms and the twin dual-diesel engines that could push the mighty ship to over twenty knots. Storage rooms filled the third level, along with a state-of-the-art infirmary and the kitchen. The crew's quarters were on the second level, each room with its own private bathroom and television. The mess hall was just below deck along with a bar and lounge straight across from the dining hall. Rescue equipment and life rafts littered the deck. They'd secured a deep-submergence vehicle to the stern of the ship by heavy chains and thick steel cables. The foredeck was mostly clear except for the Canadian flag fluttering in the wind. The bridge was two levels with a giant crow's nest stretching fifteen feet above the captain's room on the second floor.

"I will drop this equipment off on the bridge." Derrick's forearms were bulging, the sunlight shining off the layer of sweat covering them. His shoulders were tensed together as he hurried down the long corridor.

"I'm heading to my cabin." Ellen turned to leave in the opposite direction. "Once you're settled away, why don't you come see me so we can go over the plan again." Ellen winked at him.

"What room are you in again?" Andy called out.

"205."

Footsteps rocked the ramp behind Andy. He watched as Kate boarded the ship with a scowl on her face. She stormed straight past Andy and headed towards Ellen without saying a word. The ramp thumped as the Captain boarded his ship. "You must be Kevin O'Reilly," Andy said.

The young man glared at him with a disgusted look on his face. "No, Mr. O'Reilly seems to have gone into hiding. He isn't answering his phone so I'm filling in for him today." The Captain was an intimidating individual. His dark features amplified his angry snarl. "My name is Lewis Park. I'm going to be taking you out." Lewis brushed past Andy, nearly bumping into him as he hurried off towards his post. "We leave port in twenty minutes, so make sure you have everything you need. I don't plan on coming back to dock just because you're not ready."

Andy checked his watch and headed down to Ellen's room to make sure her crew had everything they needed. He was lucky enough that Derrick was able to take everything they needed in one trip. The camera crew would probably need to rush to be ready in time to leave.

Grand Banks
120 Nautical Miles South of Newfoundland

Joan's had gorged herself on the flesh of several divers, her appetite insatiable over the past few days. No matter how much she ate she couldn't satisfy her hunger. The juice from the humans was sweet, and their flesh had an awkward texture. The outer layer was troublesome to chew; she had to swallow the rubbery coating whole as she shredded the living thing's body apart. The creature's entrails were tender and rich with blood-filled organs that had left Joan wanting more. The bouquet of blood was unlike anything Joan had ever encountered. Now she scanned her head back and forth, picking up several heartbeats of the giant squids as they swam in the deeper waters off the banks' cliffs.

The *Carcharodon* was glad that her male suitors and stopped following her. The pregnant shark no longer attracted them. Her body had ceased to produce the hormone that guided them towards her. Her gills were still sore from the male shark's viscous bite marks, and the bright red wounds had grown inflamed. Her suitors now moved on towards other female sharks that had made the migration back to their ancient breeding ground. Joan needed to keep feeding in order to keep her energy levels high in the cold water. She descended into the deeper water, keeping her distance from the gathering of *Architeuthis dux*. She waited patiently for one of the squid to drift away from the others so she could isolate it and make an easy meal. She wasn't in dire need of food, her belly still full of human flesh and bones, which allowed the predator to be patient. This allowed the shark to carefully stalk her next meal, establishing her as the deadliest predator in the ocean.

200 Metres Deep
Marystown
Atlantic Ocean

Architeuthis dux began its ascent to the surface to feed. The swell of the ocean's current as the moon pulled the tide higher signaled to the creature that it was nighttime.

The waters remained cool as the fifty-foot squid rose to the surface, the jet-black waters concealing her from the view of prey along the surface. She had fled the depths since the arrival of the *Carcharodon carcharias* into its hunting grounds and was being forced to the surface to feed. Normally the creature preferred to stalk the frigid, bleak waters of the deep, concealing itself in the purgatory of the ocean depths. Lately the creature found it was able to suffer the surface waters, which had cooled considerably over the years.

The *Arcitheuthis* used its giant eye to search the surface, able to see extremely well in the moonlit waters. It would never dare surface during the daylight. The bright yellow rays hurt its eye, but the soft white light allowed it to approach the surface. In the distance a shadowy object rocked along the surface, its vibrations mimicking the fluttering muscles of an injured whale, a trail of blood in its wake.

S.S. **Harbour Delight**
Marystown
Atlantic Ocean

Madeline Northcott awoke to find that her hands had been bound by tight nylon rope, and a soiled rag filled her mouth with the bitter taste of fish guts. She tried to stand up but found out the hard way that her wrist had been bound to a board behind her back. She nearly wrenched her shoulder out of socket against the ties that bound her to the small dory. The moon hung high in the sky, its soft warm light trickling over the waves revealing the choppy waters. A brisk breeze blew foamy salt water in her face, the aroma of the deep brine alerting her that she was out in the open sea. She was a prisoner to the swell of the ocean, rising up and crashing back down like the angry heartbeat of a bull. Madeline knew once the ocean died, the entire earth would soon disintegrate in its devastating aftermath. The boards underneath her creaked and groaned as the boat bobbed up and down, the rough seas threatening to sink the smaller boat.

The last thing she recalled was standing outside of the Labyrinth Oil headquarters, pounding her fist against the door demanding an audience. She had flown into St. John's from Washington on a mission to shut down the underwater pipeline. Now she had to find a way to survive this ordeal. She forced her tongue against the rag, pushing the vile mixture of blood and fish slime down her throat. Madeline tried to suppress the urge to throw up, but her stomach muscles clenched tight as the slurry entered her guts. The vomit raced up her throat, but the gag blocked its way. The immense force had nowhere to go but out of her nose. Thick globs of bile cut off her air supply. Her chest burned as she slowly choked on it. She tried to blow her nose, but the vomit was too thick and stars quickly entered her vision.

"Not yet." A man's voice startled her from behind. A mighty hand grasped a clump of her hair. Jerking her head back he ripped out the rag. Madeline gasped at the air. She had to spit out the mouthful of vomit and fish guts before filling her lungs with large gulps of oxygen.

"What the hell are you doing to me," Madeline cried out in between heavy sobs, tears cascading down her check. She strained her neck trying to glimpse her kidnapper, but he held her at bay, pressing her neck forward and pinning her chin to her chest.

"Relax, this will all be over soon."

"You don't have to do this," Madeline pleaded.

"Well if I want to get paid then sadly, I do," the man's gruff voice answered her. "Nothing personal, just some poor life decisions I made led me down this path, but at least it pays well." He laughed anxiously.

"Please spare me." Madeline choked out her words in between sobs. "I have a family."

"What does it matter?" the man asked. "If you took your own advice, the world is ending."

"The world's not ending, just going through some violent changes," Madeline replied in a hushed tone, realizing who was behind this. Labyrinth Oil needed her silenced, and it was pointless to struggle.

"I am sorry," the man said as he propped her up. "For what it's worth, I believe in your work," the man said regrettably as he gave her a sharp push.

Madeline tumbled head over heels and plunged into the frigid waters. She instinctively tried to kick her legs but her feet had been tied together. The cold water drove the oxygen from her lungs as a fire ignited inside them. She looked up at the dying moonlight as she found herself sinking into the darkness. Tilting her head up she could see a rope stretching out from the boat that had been tied off around her waist. A sudden lurch contorted her back as the rope tightened. Her spine nearly snapped in two as she was hauled to the surface. She forced her head back as she breached the surface waters, sucking in oxygen and salty sea water. Momentarily relieving the burning sensation from her lungs, the ice-cold water number her limbs. She knew she wouldn't have long before hypothermia set in. She thought about screaming out but decided it would be best to conserve her energy, praying that the delirious man was only trying to scare her away from Labyrinth Oil.

The man peered over the edge of the skiff, his ginger beard running wild over his face. He wore a black wool knitted toque. Strands of straggly red hair fell out from underneath. "Now if you'll excuse me, I have more work to do." He dumped a bucket of fish guts and severed codfish heads over her. As the mixture poured over her, the blood was colder than the water and sent chilling shock waves throughout her body. She watched hopelessly as the man cut the thick nylon rope and started the outboard motor, the dense scent of diesel heavy in the air as black smoke spewed from the engine. The dory slowly drove out of sight. Madeline waited desperately for a miracle as her mind raced with visions of some deep sea monster below coming up to devour her. Her head slowly drifted under the water as her muscles seized up. She sank slowly at first before something below her snatched her leg in a tight vice-like grip. She looked down in horror as an impossibly long tentacle dragged her deep underneath the surface. Another tentacle appeared out of the obscurity, wrapping around her torso, taking complete control of her. A giant yellow eye slowly appeared from the darkness as the *Architeuthis* dragged her towards its snapping beak. Not waiting to feel the razor-sharp beak, Madeline opened her mouth and flooded her lungs with the ice-cold waters, praying to drown before the squid tore at her flesh.

CHAPTER SIXTEEN

Marystown
Town Wharf
The Queen Mary

Detective Shawn Bowers walked down the dock, the weathered boards groaning underneath his feet as he approached Al Patrick's berth. A twenty-five-foot schooner was anchored to the dock, the black and blue paint peeling from the hull. The name of the boat scrawled along the stern read *The Queen Mary*. Detective Bowers had taken a call from Kal Kurosawa and had greedily taken the bribe to frame the poor fisherman. He had received half of the payment into his account from an offshore company late last night, a one million dollar payment up front and another million once Al Patrick was in custody. Being a detective, he should have asked more questions, but he was desperate to retire at a young age and police work wasn't allowing him the lifestyle he had envisioned. When Shawn had first spoken to Mr. Kurosawa, he thought he would have offered a meagre bribe which he probably still would have taken, desperate for money and a one-way ticket off Newfoundland. He carried a rag covered in Madeline

Northcott's vomit; the fabric torn from her alma mater sweat shirt. In his pocket was some of Jonah McGilvery's jewelry that he wore to all of his public appearances. All he had to do was plant them on the boat before he took Al away in handcuffs, leaving the personal items behind for the other police officers to find. Mr. Kurosawa didn't care if the conviction stood, he just needed to buy himself some time to complete the pipeline.

As Shawn approached, he could see the elderly gentleman asleep in his chair through a port window, his head slumped back and to the side at a painful angle. "This is going to be much easier than I thought," Detective Bowers said out loud. He peered through the windows to get a better look. The muscles in the man's neck look like they had been stretched beyond their limits, his head weighing too much to hold up. As Shawn approached the boat, he could hear the waves slapping off its side in a relentless rhythm. He walked up the ramp that led to *The Queen Mary*, the old boards sagging down dangerously as he placed his weight on the frail structure. He reached out and grabbed the waterlogged rope that acted as a rail, preventing anyone from falling down in between the boat and the wharf.

Shawn gasped a sigh of relief as he placed his foot on the deck of the boat. He looked over his shoulder and down into the gap. The blue water looked much darker in the shadows, giving it an illusion of being much deeper than it actually was, and the short frequency of waves as they beat off the side of the wharf then the side of the boat made it look like a tempest. He crept slowly towards the captain's quarters, trying not to make any abrupt sounds as he approached the opening. A strange sound was coming from inside the enclosed cabin, an eerie sound that he couldn't identify. He laughed as the table came into view. Several empty brown beer bottles rolled back and forth with the waves. Al Patrick's filthy hands grasped a half full bottle of Jack Daniels whisky, held between his legs for better support. His green dress shirt was unbuttoned, and his sweat stained wife beater had seen better days. A putrid stench of vomit and urine caught in Shawn's throat, nearly making him puke up his coffee. Al had pissed himself sometime recently, his dingy blue jeans stained dark blue all around his crotch.

Shawn opened up a cupboard under the sink and placed Madeline's swatch of cloth under the sink, next to the bleach and cleaning supplies. Then he looked around the room, searching for a safe place to plant the jewelry before settling on the pocket of a yellow slicker that hung from an oversized screw in molding around the door. He let out a deep sigh, rationalizing that Al Patrick would be better off in jail than left to rot in this boat. The elderly fisherman was running out of time, and at least being in a cell back in St. John's he would get three square meals and a bed. Shawn took out his cell phone and called for backup.

"I need back up. I've arrested a drunken man aboard *The Queen Mary*, and I believe I may have found something."

Shawn put the phone down as the old man let out a long, anguished groan. Al batted his eyes open, squinting against the sunlight as he let out a disgusting belch. "What's goin hon ere. Who-tha fuck are ye?" Al slurred his words.

"Mr. Patrick, you are under arrest for the murder of Jonah McGilvery and Madeline Northcott." Shawn held out a pair of cuffs while hovering his hand over his service pistol, making sure that Al saw the gesture. *You're doing him a favor. The old fool doesn't know it yet, but he's better off this way.*

The Labrador Sea
Atlantic Ocean

A deep and cold water mass, the Labrador Sea is located between the Labrador Peninsula and Greenland. It was formed over sixty-million years ago, during the separation of the North American and Greenland Plates. The stretch of one-thousand kilometre sea reaches near three-thousand and four-hundred metres at its deepest depth and stays at near-freezing temperatures all year round. Nearly five-metre waves carry large icebergs down from the Arctic Ocean, making it a desolate and barren stretch of the earth's surface. People fish close to shore but avoid going out into the deeper waters.

Kevin O'Reilly woke up in a state of deep confusion, his brain throbbing against his skull as the inflamed brain matter pushed in all angles to escape the pressure. His arms and legs were bound together with thick ropes, his mouth was gagged, and his eyes were blindfolded. Kevin coughed repeatedly until the rag fell from his mouth. He sucked in large mouthfuls of fresh air, spitting out the oily sensation left behind in his mouth. He found himself unable to remember how he got here, and his body trembled with fear. The sour stench of sweat filled the air and mixed with the tangy metallic taste of hydraulic fluid. The floor of the helicopter vibrated as the blades slowed down. The change in elevation wreaked havoc on the pit of his stomach. The running boards touched down first. He had no idea where he was or how he got here. The roaring of the engine eased back, as the hiss of the hydraulics pierced deep into his skull. A metallic thud was immediately followed by a frigid gust of moist sea air. There was a taste bitter brine of salt left behind on his lips.

"Help!" Kevin cried out over the howling winds as they whistled into the cargo bay. No one responded. An ominous sound of footsteps crunching through the snow approached as someone lingered around outside.

"Please help me," Kevin begged desperately, praying for this nightmare to be over. "Why are you doing this to me?"

There was no answer. Kevin heard someone board the helicopter, their boots clunking off the metal floor as they jumped up. A powerful pair of hands grabbed him underneath the arms and dragged him away from the helicopter like a rag doll.

"Please stop this. You don't have to do this."

Bright light blinded Kevin as the blind fold was pulled down over his face, the sunlight burning through his eyelids. Squinting his eyes against the sun, Kevin saw only a silhouette of the man who stood towering over him. Once his eyes adjusted the man's features slowly came into view. The man's face was covered with a giant ginger beard that covered the neck of his jacket. His dark brown eyes stared down Kevin with a distant look to them.

"Who are you? What do you want with me?"

Kevin's antagonist reached into a breast pocket, pulling out a picture and threw it in his face. It nearly blew away with the wind, but the old Polaroid picture pinned to his chest by the steady gust. Kevin looked down to see a picture of his son and wife sitting on the living room couch. "What did you do to them?" Tears rolled down his face.

"I haven't decided yet," the man answered in a gruff voice. "That's up to you."

"I'll do anything you want, just make this stop." Kevin looked all around. The only thing visible was the rough waves and bright blue sky coming together far in the distance.

"I can spare them, but you have to agree to stay here."

"Where am I?" Kevin looked around at the sea of blue. There wasn't any land in sight.

"We are on an iceberg in the middle of the Labrador Sea. We are slowly drifting towards Newfoundland as we speak." The man took off his backpack and tossed it on the ground at Kevin's feet. "There's enough supplies in here to last you for days."

"You're fucking insane." Kevin strained against the rope, his efforts only managing to dig the fibres of the rope deep into the soft tissue of his wrist.

"I've been told you don't believe in global warming." The man let out a hearty chuckle. "And you think that I'm insane."

"What does any of this have to do with global warming?" Kevin's voice trembled, barely audible over the crashing waves as they sent tremors through the core of the iceberg.

"Nothing really. This is all about your little news clip. Labyrinth Oil is paying me to silence you, and I've just decided to get creative." The man took out a large nine-inch hunting blade. The serrated back of the knife looked like a set of razor-sharp fangs. "Normally I'd just shoot you."

"You're going to stab me to death." Kevin tried to back away, his feet slipping over the surface of the ice. He tucked his knees into the fetal position and waited for the killing blow.

"Nothing like that. Stabbing someone is too personal. I've got nothing against you so don't take this personal." The man threw the blade into the ice, the handle sticking straight up as the tip of the blade dug two inches into the thick ice with ease. "No, I'm going to leave you here on this iceberg and let science teach you one final lesson." The man knelt down and pulled the hood of his jacket over his head. His breath was heavy with the scent of coffee and cream. "Do you remember it wasn't that long ago that Newfoundland was famous for the large icebergs that would drift off our shores?"

Kevin didn't respond. He didn't know if he should make a move for the knife or take his chances in the ocean. He was paralyzed with fear, neither option giving him any hopes of survival.

"Well, thanks to global warming, most of the smaller ice floes like this will melt before it reaches the shores of Newfoundland." The man grasped the ropes that bound Kevin's hands together, yanking him forward like a rag doll. "If you make it close enough to land, you can try to swim to shore so you can warn your family. If you don't make it within five days, I'll pay that pretty little number of yours a visit."

"Fuck you. I'll never make it five days out here." Kevin spat into the man's face, the thick yellow phlegm dripping down his beard. "You have to spare my family. I'll do anything you want. Whatever they are paying you I will double it."

The man laughed hysterically as he reached for the handle of the knife. He cut the ropes with one strong movement before throwing the knife into the ocean. "You couldn't even come close to raising enough money. Trust me, I already checked into it."

"Please don't hurt my family." Kevin clasped his hands together in front of his face, pleading with the mad man.

"Maybe I will, maybe I won't. I just want you to think about it as you're out here drifting towards Newfoundland. It should take about four or five days depending on the currents. They are pretty slow now, but the wind has been picking up." The man kicked the giant bag that he had thrown on the ground. "Everything you need to survive for five days is in here."

"This is insane. You can't leave me here like this to die," Kevin called out as the man walked back towards the helicopter.

"You wouldn't be the first Newfoundlander to be left alone to die on the ice floes." The man jumped into the cockpit. Kevin tried to jump to his feet, but the ropes tripped him up, and he fell hard into the ice. His face smashed against the solid surface, a gush of blood pouring from his nose as he looked up at the helicopter blades gaining speed. Kevin reached down to untie the rope from his legs. The knots pulled into tight bundles making it near impossible to free from his legs.

Kevin eased himself to his feet, the warm feeling of blood running down his face made him sick. He could taste the coppery fluid as it dribbled over his lips and into his dry mouth. The helicopter lifted off from the iceberg as Kevin watched hopelessly. The aircraft got smaller and smaller as it faded away into the horizon.

Kevin sat down beside the duffle bag and unzipped it. A yellow Gor-Tex coat lined with faux fur was laid on top. Kevin pulled it over his shoulders and zipped it up. The jacket blocked the wind from chilling his bones, and he could feel the warmth quickly building inside. The stranger had stuffed a green knitted hat and a pair of green waterproof gloves into the pockets to help keep him protected from the wet weather. Bottles of water and brown paper bags filled with rations had been stuffed into the bag along with a Coleman stove. Kevin lay down on his back and stared up at the sun as he drifted along with the Labrador Current, basking in the sun's warm glow. His whole body shivered violently as the cold water from the melting iceberg seeped into his jeans. Kevin didn't know if he would make it through the night. He sat up and fumbled with the ropes. he worked patiently to free his legs. He didn't know how much longer this iceberg would last. He needed to be ready to swim for it.

CHAPTER SEVENTEEN

CCGS Heart's Content
42 Nautical Miles East of Cape Race

Andy looked at the chalkboard outside of the mess hall. He couldn't decide between the deep-fried cod and chips or the calamari rings for supper. The waves had been treacherous as the giant swells slowed the voyage, already putting them behind schedule. Derrick and Ellen had already grabbed their meals and were sat at a table with Kate, chatting about the wicked weather. "I'll have the calamari." Andy watched as the server ceremoniously dumped a scoop of the squid rings onto a plate. The worker pointed towards two large silver containers filled with fries or mashed potato, the staples of any sea voyage. "Potato please."

Andy walked over to the massive stainless-steel cooler to grab a bottle of water and a bowl of pudding for his dessert. He joined the others, sliding his tray across the table as he sat down. The waves rolled endlessly outside of the port window. Rough whitecaps peaked at the crest of the wave before rushing down into the valley's below. "So, have you been able to get the satellite tag up and running yet, Derrick?" Andy asked.

Derrick looked over at Andy with an annoyed look plastered on his face. "I did actually, no thanks to you."

"Sorry, Derrick, I made him stay behind to organize what the cameras were going to film," Ellen said, defending Andy. "We need to know what to be looking for."

Derrick stabbed his fries with his fork. "Whatever. I mean it's all set up now so I think I'll be heading down for a nap. I'm sick to my stomach." Derrick stood up and nearly lost his balance as the ship rolled forty degrees to the port side. His utensils flew off his tray and skittered across the fibreglass floor. He reached out and clutched the bench. "I'm still not sure why I need to be on this damned ship. It would have been the same if I set up on land and radioed you."

Andy felt bad for making Derrick board the CCGS *Heart's Content*. "I thought you'd be alright on this ship. It's much larger than the ones we are used to," Andy apologized.

Derrick waited by the table for a moment, waiting for his legs to adjust to the sway of the giant vessel. "If you need me, I'll be in my room." Derrick walked away from the table, grabbing onto the back of other people's chairs with every change of direction.

"I guess that's the reason I always found him in the tent," Ellen tried to joke, but Andy sympathized with Derrick.

"I haven't seen the seas this rough in a long time." Kate changed the subject. "Must be a storm approaching fast. Maybe we should consider heading back to port."

"This vessel was designed to operate in these conditions." Ellen was determined not to lose any more time. "We will reach the Grand Banks soon and once we get some footage of a pregnant shark; you can run back to your little classroom."

"Your documentary is pandering to the lowest common denominator," Kate retorted. "No offence, Andy."

Andy sensed the tension between the two ladies. Both of them were trying to show their superiority over the other. "Listen, as long as the captain keeps this ship out here, we must be safe. He isn't going to put us all in danger."

"Lewis is a fool." Kate snapped.

"So, you two do have a history. I guess that's the real reason you want off this boat." Ellen leaned back in her chair and giggled.

"None of your business."

"Alright, you two, there is no reason to be at each other's throats." Andy wanted to defuse the situation. "We've only been out here for four hours. We are going to have to work together." The three of them sat at the dinner table in silence. The waves ravaging the side of the boat, crashing into the hull with a thunderous roar. Vibrations ran through the entire ship. Andy watched the tiny ripples in his bottle of water.

"Do you mind if I sit with you." Lewis Park stood at the head of the table holding his tray with both hands.

"Please be my guest." Ellen offered him a seat much to Kate's dismay.

"So, is this weather going to force us to turn back?" Andy asked, ignoring the tension between Lewis and Kate.

"This ship was built to handle anything the ocean can throw at it," Lewis responded as if by automated response. "We wouldn't be able to do our job if it wasn't." Lewis let out cocky laugh.

Ellen leaned far back in her seat, stretching her arms above her head as she yawned. "These waves aren't even that bad. I wouldn't say they are over ten feet."

"The waves have been peaking at just over fifteen feet," Lewis added as he took a bite of battered fish.

Kate pulled her chair out and stood up. "Andy, I'd like to discuss your method of tagging sharks." She picked up her empty tray, her glass nearly toppling over.

Andy looked down at his plate and stuck his fork in the powdered potatoes. "Just let me finish up and I'll meet you on the bridge."

"I will be in my room." Kate winked at Andy as she brushed past Lewis. Giving Andy a sly glance as she walked away.

"How much longer until we reach our destination?" Andy asked.

Lewis checked his watch. "I'd say we got at least another four hours or more unless this weather eases up."

Andy took a bit of the flavourless potato mash and stared out at the pitch-black storm clouds approaching from the south. A thunderous boom rolled across the vast ocean, announcing the brooding clouds were ready to burst open. The ominous clouds outside block out the day's light, casting the sky in a premature twilight. Far in the distance a bolt of hot white light split the horizon in half, illuminating the giant waves as they rolled over each other. Thick sheets of rain poured from the sky, the bright white lights of the CCGS *Heart's Content* catching the rain drops in a brilliant display of mother nature's immense power. A flash river formed on the decks as the rain water gushed over the sides and down the windows.

"This storm looks bad. We won't be able to get much of a signal until the weather passes." Andy stood up to leave.

"I'll catch up with you." Ellen brushed Andy off as she rubbed her foot up Lewis's leg.

Andy walked away before his facial expressions betrayed his attempt to hide his jealousy. "Yeah, I'll see you on the bridge when the storm passes." Andy swayed back and forth, the sea rising like a great mountain underneath him. The water was turbulent and unforgiving as if it were angry. As he walked past the window, he witnessed flashes of bright white light on the dark horizon and the gregarious roar of booming thundering approaching them. Gale force winds carried salt water in the air sideways, the rain drops pelting against the hull of the ship. Andy decided that he would join Kate below deck to pass the time. He needed to distract himself from Ellen. His blood pressure rose. He acted like she was betraying him again. He cursed himself for not making a move earlier.

Joan of Shark
500 meters deep
Twelve nautical miles south of the Grand Banks
Jolts of dynamic electrical impulses jarred the great white's ampullae of Lorenzini, briefly overloading her senses with every strike. With every bolt of lightning the jarring force scrambled Joan's senses like a blow to

the head. Mother nature forced the *Carcharodon carcharious* to dive deeper and deeper, abandoning her quest for food. Normally she would be able to pinpoint a single fish amongst a school, but the electrical overload fried her navigational senses. Joan still sensed the tremendous surges rushing through the ocean even at depths of five-hundred metres, forcing her to keep diving further down in a rush.

She hastily dove to seven-hundred metres to escape the overbearing signals. The inky black waters were filled with fantastic creatures. Prehistoric lifeforms adapted to life without light by developing the ability to produce light through a chemical reaction called bioluminescence. Different species of fish used the light in different ways. Several species of squid used this light to camouflage with the overhead light so they couldn't be seen from below. Some fish like the angler fish used it to lure their prey while others used it to attract a mate. Any of these tactics should not fool the great white shark. The creature's heartbeat gave away its position, but her senses still hadn't recovered from the overload of electrical impulses. The lightening from the surface no longer bothered Joan, but it forced her into danger. Before she could react, the long tentacle of a fifty-foot *Architeuthis dux* wrapped around her torso. The suction cups allowed the squid to gain a tight grip on her before she could swim out of the arms' reach.

The giant squid wrapped another suction-filled tentacle around Joan and began to pull its body towards her. Joan thrashed her tail fin and forced all of her energy into her muscular body in an attempt to sever her attacker's grip. The shark was able to pull the *Architeuthis* through the deep ocean waters with her but couldn't shake the creature's tentacles from her body. With every fleeting moment the squid managed to tighten its vice-like grip on its prey, its giant black eye staring at Joan intently. Joan had to keep moving. It was the only way she could keep breathing. She changed direction abruptly and hurtled her pyramidal nose into her assailant, generating as much force as a head on collision between two cars. The massive *Architeuthis* was caught off guard by the shark's powerful blow. The vice-like grips of its tentacle that had once been its greatest weapon would now spell the creature's doom. The suction cups couldn't let go of Joan soon enough, as her jaw jutted forward into the squid. A row of three-inch razor-sharp teeth sliced into the squid's soft flesh, tearing it apart with ease. Trying desperately to escape, the giant squid tore its tentacles from its own body as the shark continued to chomp into its flesh. Her mouth opening and closing, pieces of shredded flesh and dark blood spilled out from Joan's mouth.

Joan felt the lifeless tentacles slowly fall away from her body, leaving behind bright red circles from the powerful suckers. She swam back up to six-hundred metres with her mouth left slightly ajar in an evil grin, her jaw spasming as the water flushed through her gills once more. She could sense the powerful heartbeat of another squid nearby amongst the flutter of a school of smaller fish. Too exhausted from her fight and mentally drained from the storm, Joan kept her distance from the squid and the surface. The strikes of lightning on the surface were hitting faster now as the storm was passing directly overhead.

CCGS Heart's Content
Twenty-nine Nautical Miles South East of Cape Race

Andy knocked on the door, the shallow drumming echoing down the hallway. He heard Kate shuffling her feet across the floor, the door latch sliding open just before the door creaked open. Kate had let her hair down, the long strands of golden-brown hair falling over her shoulders. "Come in." Holding open the door, Kate removed her university sweater. Underneath she was wearing a charcoal grey tee shirt. She had tucked one side into her jeans while letting the other side hang loosely over her hip.

Andy stepped inside the cramped quarters and pulled out the single chair by the side of the bed. "Thanks."

Kate walked over and sat on the edge of her single bed. "I can't believe how quickly this storm sprang up." A steady flash of bright light lit up the dark waves outside the tiny porthole of her berth. "I don't remember the weatherman saying anything about this storm on the evening weather."

"They were too busy reporting on the whale carcass to worry about the weather." Andy recalled the weatherman bumbling through the weather, still rattled by the discovery of sharks shredding apart the dead humpback whale.

"I meant the university sonar station," Kate giggled. "I never listen to that guy, anyway."

"I've never seen waves so big before in all my life," Andy said as a wave rocked the boat, rattling the entire steel hull. "This is getting crazy. I'm just waiting for the captain to bring us back to port."

"Yeah, he won't be doing that. He's got too much to

prove." Kate's voice was bitter and full of resentment.

"So, you two obviously have a history," Andy prodded, hoping for an interesting story or anything that would help pass the time.

Kate looked down at her feet. "We used to date before." Her voice was low, the pounding raindrops making it difficult for Andy to hear her. "I thought it was serious, but I guess I was wrong."

Andy stared straight ahead, not knowing what to say. He heard the hurt pouring out, but she didn't seem to want to elaborate. For several minutes they sat in silence, the raging storm outside offering enough distraction between them to not make it awkward. The cracking claps of thunder and howling hiss of the wind roared over the open ocean. Magnificent waves had their way with the forty-eight foot search and rescue ship. Through the tiny porthole, the sky vanished behind giant towering walls of water. Thick lines of white foam whirled around in the waves like spiderwebs. Every time the boat crested a wave the entire ship would be rocked violently as the nose dove back down into the next valley, the next wave slamming hard against the ship.

The sudden sound of the door opening to the adjacent berth startled both of them. Andy overheard Ellen talking to someone. He wanted to press his ear against the thin wall to hear what she was saying but wasn't sure how Kate would react. Thankfully Kate was just as interested as he was when a deep voice responded to Ellen. Kate leaned back on her elbows, the back of her head resting against the wall. The sound of heavy breathing and fumbling against the furniture brought a flustered expression to her face, and Andy felt his heart sinking into the pit of his stomach. The groans and moans grew louder, escalating quickly in Ellen's room.

"Would you like to grab a drink?" Kate stood up from the bed quickly as the entangled bodies fell into the bed, the frame thudding off the wall.

"What are the chances they're serving in this storm?" Andy asked before he caught on to the meaning of her question. She didn't care what they did, she just wanted to leave. Andy wasn't stupid but knew that he didn't want to stick around much longer either. "Let's go see."

They left Kate's room in a hurry. The sounds of Ellen's passionate moans spilled into the hallway as they rushed towards the exit. Andy turned the corner, trying his best to push the sounds out of his mind, but he still heard them no matter how hard he tried to shake it. He was jealous and furious at the same time. he wanted to break down the door and demand an answer from Ellen. He truly believed they had been hitting it off since the plane ride back from Africa, but he couldn't understand how quickly she threw herself at Lewis. He cursed at himself under his breath. They walked past the entrance to the dining hall and just a little further down at the end of the hallway were two giant double wooden doors with large brass handles. Andy checked the door handle. Relieved to find it unlocked, he held the door open for Kate.

The sharp smell of liquor wafted through the room, mixed with the stench of sick. The only reason the bar was open was to give access to the bathrooms. Andy could hear groans as people heaved their guts up from behind closed doors. Behind the teak bar there were only two shelves that had been stacked with every hue of amber liquid. Andy was glad to see members of the film crew sprawled out on the giant leather couches, their skin as pale as ghosts. A trio of dartboards lined the back wall covered in red and green patterns. There was a pool table in the corner, the balls clanking off each other with the sway of the boat in a never ending racket. The floor boards were made from light hardwood and given a sophisticated shine. All the furniture was made to resemble vintage pieces, like it had been pulled from the Titanic. The Victorian era pieces looked expensive and brand new. The colors were bright and vibrant, the fabrics spotless and plush looking.

"Swanky." Andy was shocked by how big the bar on the search and rescue ship was. "I've never seen such a large bar on a search and rescue ship."

"Yeah this is the government pissing away money trying to appear better off than they actually are," Kate replied with a disheartened tone. "They purchased this craft from a New Zealand cruise line company in order to save money."

"Where do you want to sit?" Andy asked as he scoured the room looking for a quiet place to talk. They spotted a leather love seat unoccupied behind a wooden coffee table and headed over. Andy sank into the soft cushion, the air seeping from underneath him slowly, lowering him down towards the floor. Kate sat down next to him; her leg pressed against his sending a warm tingle racing through his body. "I can't believe they didn't convert this into something more practical, but it is a beautiful place to come relax after a long day's work at sea."

"This ship is the one they use to entertain dignities

that visit the island." Kate placed her hands in her lap, her fingers nervously fiddling with each other. "A false showcase of how well off the government is in this province."

"That seems like a huge waste of money for no reason." Andy leaned back, questioning himself about putting an arm around her but wasn't sure if he should.

"The government here likes to pretend we are doing better than we are, but they are nothing more than a bunch of crooks. Instead of getting something we needed, we asked for an outlandish ship to show off." Kate complained as she leaned into Andy, pressing hard against him as the boat began to change direction. The waves tilted the boat at thirty-degree angles as it glided up and down with each swell. She reached out to brace herself, her hand falling on his knees. "We must be making our way out towards the Grand Banks now," she said. Andy's stomach contents were rolling with the ship, the waves getting larger now as they entered the eye of the storm. He braced himself against the arm of the sofa, allowing Kate to fall into him with every crash of the stern. He embraced her toned, warm body as it pressed against his muscular frame. He fought the urge to puke his guts up, desperately wanting to stay on the couch with Kate he swallowed back a mouthful of bile.

The CCGS *Heart's Content* headed into the gale force winds head on. The twin engine ship struggled to stay on course as the wind buffeted the ship one way then the next. Outside, the wind continued to howl, pelting the window with rain mercilessly. The engines groaned under the pressure, billowing out two black plumes of diesel smoke behind her. The entire boat creaked as the wind relentlessly battered and tore at every crevice of the ship as it growled with the violence and raw power of Poseidon himself. The booming thunder cracked overhead with virtually no break, the flashes of lightening streaking through the sky.

"I'm going to be sick." Andy tried to stand up, but the boat rocked hard forcing him back down. He tucked his head between his legs, hoping that the nausea would pass.

Kate rubbed his back gently, her hands pressing lightly just between his shoulder blades. "You'll be fine. Just focus on the floor. Don't look out the window," Kate spoke calmly.

"How can you handle this?" Andy asked as he tucked his knees closer together. He had grown up on the ocean and spent most of his waking hours on a boat, but he had never gotten seasick before.

"I've grown accustomed to the harsh weather off our coast," Kate said gently. "This will pass soon enough."

Andy groaned in agony as the hull shuddered. He felt Kate's arm reach out and guide his head into her lap. "Just close your eyes and try not to think about it." She ran her fingers through his hair trying to soothe him. "So, tell me, how did you manage to get your own television show?"

"Well that's a long story." Andy swung his legs over the arm of the sofa, looking up at Kate. Her hair veiled her face as she stared out to the sea.

"Well we got nothing else to do, unless you have something better in mind?"

Momentarily forgetting about Ellen and Lewis, Andy could think of other things to do to pass the time, but the weather prevented him from making any moves. "I remember you suggesting this will pass soon."

Kate smiled. "You probably have time for one story."

Andy felt safe in Kate's lap. He focused on her slate-blue eyes and pushed out everything else. "Well, when I was working on my thesis for school, I invented a device that would deter sharks from populated beaches. I used underwater acoustic speakers to play orcas singing to each other. Great white sharks avoided killer whales because they had recently begun to feed on their livers."

"I heard about that. You set those up on the beaches of South Africa." Kate smiled as she looked down at Andy. "So, why don't we use your device in North America?"

Andy could sense the sea sickness passing as he lost himself in conversation. "As I'm sure you know, the *Carcharodon carcharias* have evolved differently all around the world. Whites in African waters hunt in murkier water than those on the western coast of California. They have acquired particular techniques to ambush their prey. They also face different enemies. Killer whales only hunted the sharks near the shores of Africa, so the great whites near California were not programmed to fear the orcas. We tried to use my method to deter them on the beaches of California, but it failed."

"So, your failure landed you a television show?" Kate looked perplexed.

Andy chuckled. "It was a scientific breakthrough. We discovered that we could assign subgenus classifications to the distinctive types of *Carcharodon*. That and the boat-load of money I made from the government of South Africa allowed me enough popularity and the means to fund my own research. The university loved me and thrust money at me, and the rest they say is history."

"I've watched your show a few times. I must say you're a better palaeobiologist than an actor." Kate grinned from ear to ear.

"Geez thanks, I guess." Andy closed his eyes as Kate played with his hair and the waves grew so large, they dwarfed the vessel. The storm showed no mercy. There was no grace in the waves only wrath and tempest. Andy felt comfortable in Kate's arms. "Can I tell you something I've never told anyone else?"

Kate let out a soft groan. "Sure, I mean I didn't realize this was an episode of *Degrassi High*, but if that's what floats your boat."

"Maybe I don't want to tell you now." Andy became defensive, sitting up and turning to face Kate. Her slate-blue eyes and wide grin allowed him to relax again.

"Oh, come on. I was only kidding," Kate pleaded, clasping her hands together in front of her chest, pretending to beg.

Andy laid back down. "It's about what I did before I got involved in all of this pageantry." Andy paused, building up the courage to continue. "I used to be a clearance diver with the Navy."

"Really?" Kate sounded surprised. "No offence, but I would have never pegged you as being patriotic.

"My job was to clear explosives we found underneath the water." Andy choked back an anguished cry; his throat as dry as sandpaper. "One day I was so intoxicated I could barely function, but I still cleared myself for duty. I found the explosive device and determined that it wasn't in our direct path. I told my superiors I deactivated the bomb, thinking we would avoid any danger."

"Did the ship change course?" Kate asked, invested in the story.

"No, we made it to port with no incident just as I predicted."

"Then what happened?"

"A research vessel charted by a high school science group passed us as we entered port. The scientists were showing the teenagers how to tag great white sharks in an effort to get them interested in a career in marine biology." Andy paused, warm tears rolling down his cheeks as he remembered his commander calling him into the office. "They hit the explosive device I said I deactivated. No one survived. I received a dishonourable discharge from the Navy."

Kate wiped away a tear from Andy's face. "I don't know what to say."

"You don't have to say anything." Andy closed his eyes. "Every time I enter the water with those sharks, I pray one of them will end my suffering."

The Labrador Sea
Atlantic Ocean

The piping hot yellow sun beat down on Kevin, sweat dripping down his backside. Looking down at his feet, he watched helplessly as tiny rivers of melting water flushed from the iceberg into the ocean. The sun was relentless in its attempt to melt the massive hunk of ice. Kevin couldn't sit down because the flood-waters were much too cold. His leg muscles were getting sore from standing in place, the surface much too slippery to walk around. His feet ached from the ice-cold waters that soaked through his boots and drenched his socks. It was amazing that he found himself so hot and cold at the same time. It brought with it a sense of dread.

A gale force wind threw the cold waters of the ocean into his face with a furious rage, the waves rocking the mighty iceberg in the rough current. The bright horizon began slowly fading away as the sun dropped beneath the water, casting looming shadows across the ocean. Kevin's mind raced with fear. He didn't know if he was more afraid of drowning or freezing to death. He remembered how his grandmother used to tell him stories about how her grandfather had been left behind on the ice floes during a winter storm to die during the great sealing disaster of 1914. He lost most of his fingers and toes to an extreme case of frostbite before he fell through the ice. Kevin began to imagine he would soon experience exactly how much his great grandfather suffered that day.

Kevin shuddered. Ominous grey clouds rolled in towards him far in the distance, bringing a brisk wind with them. He wasn't able to judge how much longer it would be until the storm reached him, but the atmosphere was already changing around him. The wind whipped into his face, carrying a chill with it. The vast storm front stretched across the whole horizon to the south, the creeping shadow heading his way. Unable to find any sign of land in any direction, his only hope was that the storm would miss him as it swept over the ocean.

His heart beat faster and faster and he started to hyperventilate. He sat down to catch his breath, the cold waters soaking through his jeans, sending a chill throughout his body. Kevin didn't want to face a night out on the open ocean in a storm with no shelter. Kevin lay back. A pool of bitter cold water pooled underneath him. His body shook uncontrollably as his muscles fought against the cold, his brain suppressing the instinct to move. He closed his eyes to wait for the cold to take him away.

CHAPTER EIGHTEEN

The Labrador Sea
Atlantic Ocean

Ice cold ice pellets tore at the skin on Kevin's exposed cheeks. He tried to open his eyes, but his tears had frozen them shut once the sun had disappeared beneath the waves. He tried to move his hands, but the muscles in his arms were numb. A thousand ice cold needles pierced his body sending shock waves of pain racing to his brain. He tried to kick his legs, but his feet were encased in ice. The melted water had refrozen and trapped him against the ice flow. He knew he should have been cold, but his body wasn't shivering anymore; his muscles had all but given up. He squeezed his eyes shut and tried opening them several times before the thin layer of ice finally broke. The perfectly dark sky was littered with a thousand white specks. A full moon above cast a shimmer across the waves. All he saw above his head was a clear night sky. He didn't see any clouds even though it was hailing.

Kevin tried to scream for help, but his throat was too dry. His tongue was glued to the roof of his mouth. He tried to make enough saliva to wet his tongue, the lump of flesh nearly choking out his air supply. Desperately wishing this was some terrible nightmare, he closed his eyes once more praying that he would slip back into a deep sleep. Kevin found no comfort. His backside was rubbed raw. Huge blisters had formed from the rough ice that glued him to the ice floe as the waves rattled the chunk of ice back and forth. He couldn't feel his toes. He tried to wiggle them but nothing happened. Images of his family raced through his mind. Horrible images of them dying in their own personal hell played against the back of his eyelids. The mad man who had left him to die on the ice floe had learned about his own opinion on the effects of global warming, punishing him ironically with death by the bold statement. His wife was deathly afraid of fires, and he worried that she would be burned alive. His son was deathly afraid of heights. He pictured him dangling from a tall building, suspended precariously from a rope that would give away at any moment.

"Hello."

A distant voice carried on the wind. Kevin opened his eyes and stared off into the oblivion of space. He moved his head to the left, his hair ripping from his head as it tore from the ice. All that remained in his field of vision was the flicker of moonlight kissing the crests of the waves. He rolled his head to the other side in one painful movement, but there was only emptiness no matter where he looked. He must have imagined the voice.

"Are you alive?"

The voice sounded closer now, more familiar than it was before. Kevin tried to clear his throat. A giant lump formed in his swollen throat. With his mouth wide open, he let the ice pellets fall into his mouth and melt inside.

"H… H… HE… Help." Kevin's dry voice cracked.

"Hello."

Kevin forced his arms to move, digging his elbows into the hard surface. He pushed down with all of his might, the skin tearing off his back as he pressed himself up. A painful yelp escaped his lips, tears streaming down his face. "Help me! I'm over here!" Kevin screeched.

"Can you get to me?"

Kevin looked in all directions but couldn't spot the woman's voice. "Please help me!" Kevin cried. Deep sobs cut his sentence into smaller chunks. Looking down at his hands, Kevin nearly vomited at his blackened fingers. The skin looked like it had been burnt in a fire and hurt just as bad. Kevin looked at the ice below him. The tip of his nose had fallen off his face and was stuck in the ice. "Just get me out of here," Kevin begged.

"You have to get up."

"I can't get up!" Kevin screamed in frustration.

"You have to keep us safe."

The voice screamed in his ears.

"This is your fault."

Kevin heard his wife's anguished cry, her calls for help choked with tears. "Amy, where are you." He frantically searched the vast ocean, the delirium setting in now.

"We are down here."

Kevin tried to stand up, but he had no sensation in his feet. He tripped up in his boots and tumbled down the slippery slope of the iceberg, the frigid waters rushing towards him to greet him. He plummeted into the sea face first, the world going completely dark as the jet-black waters engulfed him. The cold no longer affected him, but the salt water stung his eyes as he searched for his family. Kevin's arms and legs felt like cement as he tried move. He drifted deep below the surface. His lungs burned for oxygen. From the depths, Kevin heard Amy laughing maniacally. He opened his mouth to scream. What little air he had left escaped his lips and floated towards the surface, the salty water filling his lungs as he began his descent to the ocean floor.

CHAPTER NINETEEN

Joan of Shark
Four-hundred metres deep
Eight nautical miles south of the Grand Banks

Joan swam through the calming waters in a catatonic state, the closest thing nature would allow to sleep for the *Carcharodon*. Half of her brain rested as her pectoral fins kept rigid and stuck straight out by her sides to keep her upright, her mighty tail fin swaying side to side pushing the ocean waters through her gills. A vast change in her surroundings stirred her to wake. The animal lived her life in a constant state of movement, always pushing forward. Instincts guided the shark from one meal to the next, her stomach and brain linked together by the ocean's most complex nervous system.

The surge of electrical energy slowly rolled past, allowing Joan to venture closer to the surface. Surrounded by ink-black waters, Joan saw the ocean as a vivid map, the beating hearts sending bright signals to the shark's peppered black snout. Water rushed into Joan's golf-ball-sized nostrils, the bouquet of diesel fuel and smoke running through her nose. A giant vibrating source of electrical impulses on the surface caught her attention. The dull sounds of the creaking boat mimicked the sound of a dying whale. With a strong thrust of her tail, Joan changed directions quickly to investigate the disturbance. As she rose from the depths, the ocean changed from a deep violet into an emerald green as rays of sunlight reached out for Joan.

She scaled the rocky sea cliff at the edge of the drop-off that reached up from the depths. It was broken by fissures and caves that were inhabited by seaweed, kelp, and small fish that hid from predators in the tight confines in the rock. The bright morning sun had began to rise high into the sky, the storm clouds vanishing from view. As Joan approached the surface, she still sensed the static electricity left behind from the lightening last night. The ocean currents had returned to normal as the waves died down, letting Joan cruise through the waves with ease as her caudal fin cut through the surface.

A mighty heartbeat caught Joan's attention. The pulse was strong but calm; she turned her snout towards the beating muscles. As the water flushed into her nostrils, she could smell the predator; it was another female *Carcharodon*. All of Joan's senses alerted her to stay away. The vibrations she felt in her lateral line dwarfed even the largest whale she had ever stalked. The hormones that the female produced warned Joan to stay away, and she changed direction immediately. Her motherly instincts took over allowing her to quickly realize she would stand no chance against this new predator in the waters.

CCGS **Heart's Content**
Atlantic Ocean
Cliffs of the Grand Banks

Andy awoke to the rapid boom of hammering at his door. His stomach was still nauseous from the storm, but the gigantic waves had long died out. The knocking continued. The sharp pounding seemed in sync with the pulsing in his temples. "Who is it?" Andy groaned as the knocking grew louder.

"It's Ellen." Andy sensed the irritable manner of her voice through the door. "We're here. You need to get in the water now."

Deep down he had hoped it was Kate. Ellen was the last person he wanted to see right now. He rubbed his head, trying to comprehend getting into the water. "Did Derrick pick up Joan's signal?"

"Listen, we don't have time for this. The film crew is waiting and there's no way we are missing this." Ellen forced her way through the unlocked door. Her black hair was glued to her forehead, matted into clumps. A harsh light from the fluorescent bulb gleamed off the sweat on her forehead. She had on an oversized sweater. The neck was much too large for her, showing off the white flesh of her cleavage. Ellen must have sensed Andy's eyes lingering, she tugged at the neck to adjust the neckline. "Come on, we can't afford to miss this."

"I've seen a dead whale before." Andy swung his legs around, letting his bare feet touch the cold floor. He thought about protesting, but he knew Ellen wasn't going to let up. He had already convinced her to travel all the way to Newfoundland, and he wasn't about to press his luck. "What's the big deal," he pouted.

"Just throw on your wetsuit and meet us on deck." Ellen disappeared down the corridor before Andy had the chance to say anything else.

Rummaging through his messy suitcase, he found the vacuum sealed pouch that contained his wetsuit. It was constructed to withstand near-freezing temperatures and contained an electrical current that would distort his pulse from the ampullae of Lorenzini of the great white. He stripped off his sweat-soaked boxers and used a towel to dry off his body, making it easier to slip into his suit. Once he dried off, he put on clean underwear and socks. Stepping into the suit he pulled the arms up over his shoulders and wiggled his body to squeeze into the wetsuit. He grabbed his flippers and rushed down the hallway, fighting the urge to knock on Kate's door as he sprinted past.

As Andy opened the door, he couldn't help but notice the sky was glowing pink with hints of orange hues trying to push its way through the beautiful backdrop. The sun rose into the air like a burning ember shooting from a fire, its orange glow shining fiercely. The deck of the *Heart's Content* was buzzing with activity as the film crew eased the silver metal shark cage into the waters, making sure it didn't get entangled into the side of the coast guard ship or any of the wires that ran along the deck. Ellen stood near the edge of the rail holding a hand-held camera and a snorkel. She waved at him, her hands flailing frantically trying to catch Andy's attention. "Hurry up before we lose the shot."

Andy obeyed. Preferring not to have to look for a new career, he jogged over the wet deck, his bare feet slapping off the metal surface. As he approached the rail, he detected a hint of the rotting whale carcass on the breeze. He heard the water splashing all around as he saw the dorsal fins slicing through the water around the dead mammal. "Jesus Christ," Andy muttered out loud, his jaw gaping open at the ferocity below. He had never seen so many great white sharks at the surface at the same time.

"You sure you want to go out there with them all riled up like that?" Lewis cried out from above.

"He'll be fine in the steel cage," Ellen answered for him.

Andy's heart was racing, the adrenaline coursing through his veins as Ellen thrust the snorkel into his chest. "I'm not confident that I'm ready to do this?" He searched around for Kate, suddenly feeling the desire to say goodbye to her.

"Once people experience this footage, they will be all over you. You'll be a superstar. We won't have to worry about money anymore," Ellen said enthusiastically.

"What do you mean *we*?" Andy let the last word hang from his lips, questioning the interpretation of Ellen's definition of the term. It was only a few hours ago that Andy pictured them as a couple, but the man standing above him put that image in serious jeopardy. Did she mean business partners? A fury of emotions ran through his brain in a dash. Before he got a reply from Ellen, someone spun him around.

"Come on, before I lose my nerves." Derrick took the camera from Ellen in his giant hand making it look like a child play toy.

"Wait, what about the cameraman?" Andy questioned

"Are you fucking nuts?" one of the crew piped up. "No way I'm getting into that water with all those fucking sharks."

Andy stared at Ellen. The pink glow of the sky behind her made her appear even more beautiful than he had ever seen her before. Her bronzed skin and pale blue eyes basked in the radiating glow of the majestic morning sky. Andy spit into his mask, allowing him to get a better seal. He climbed over the rail of the *Heart's Content* and eased himself down to the cage without speaking to her. Derrick quickly followed behind him. As Andy opened the top of the cage and climbed into the ice-cold waters of the Atlantic Ocean, all he could think about was the old saying his father would say.

Pink sky at night, sailors delight
Pink sky at morning, sailors take warning

Andy kept telling himself he wasn't a sailor. He was a scientist, and he didn't believe in old proverbs. The colour of the sky had no bearing on the situation. The sky may as well have been bright blue. Either way it was a treacherous and stupid idea to climb into an untested cage with a herd of savage *Carcharodon*.

Shark Cage
Atlantic Ocean
Cliffs of the Grand Banks

As the cage lowered in the frigid waters of the Atlantic Ocean, Andy discovered the phenomenon of claustrophobia for the first time in the water. The pen had hardly plunged five feet below the surface, the blazing orange tinge of the sun still visible, but Andy found himself trapped inside those steel bars. He was sequestered in obscurity, inserted in an underwater prison cell with Derrick, powerless to communicate verbally with the man who was swimming shoulder to shoulder with him. As his eyes adjusted to the murky waters, the horrific scene folded out before him, making the cage resemble the gates to hell. Tiny steel bars were the sole defence from the snapping jaws waiting to twist his cage into his coffin.

Derrick reached out and patted Andy on the shoulder then pointed to the red light on the camcorder and gave him a thumbs up. Andy quickly reciprocated the gesture, taking his cue that he was now on camera. Andy began by pointing out an eighteen-foot great white shark as it swam past their cell not more than fifteen feet away. Its powerful body propelled the beast through the rough waters with practiced ease. The *Carcharodon* was forcing its way straight for the shredded whale carcass, joining in on the smorgasbord of whale blubber. Six sharks of approximately equal magnitude had already staked their seat at the dinner table, their razor-sharp teeth buried into the dead whale's flesh. As the eighteen-footer rammed its snout into the humpback whale, its body rattled from the impact as the powerful shark drove away its competition. Derrick panned the camera around, noticing at least another dozen great whites coming towards the whale from all angles. Andy looked down at his feet as a powerful current swept underneath. The largest *Carcharodon carcharias* that he had ever seen emerged from the depths. Its jaws must have been at least four-feet wide, its jagged white teeth a terrifying exhibit of its pure ferocity. Its grey back was littered with deep scars that had vivid red rivers running in their depths, its white snout peppered with black dots and two tangerine-sized nares. The horrifying form rose from the shadows. Andy's eyes grew wide and his heart skipped a beat as the impressive anatomy kept forming from the blackness, the cold dead eyes glaring at him as it rose. Its pectoral fins must have spanned ten feet as the trunk continued to widen. The jagged dorsal fin stood four feet from its spin hinting at the *Carcharodon's* advanced age. The body slowly began to thin as the pelvic fin emerged before the seven-foot caudal fin finally came into view.

The great white shark must have been at least twenty-five feet from the tip of its snout to its mighty caudal fin that swayed with an effortless motion. With ease the great white flexed its muscles, thrusting the shark forward as if on autopilot. The cage swayed in it its wake as the shark swam past; it headed for the humpback to claim its meal. The other sharks backed away from the feast as the shark clamped its mighty jaws into the flesh of the whale. The ancient predator's massive girth dragged the whale underneath the water as it thrashed its head side to side. The humpback popped back up to the surface as a four-hundred pound hunk of whale blubber tore off its frame. The massive female shark circled near her dinner, chewing greedily on her meal.

The other great whites started to circle closer to the cage making sure to keep their distance. They waited for the alpha shark to have her fill before they attempted to rejoin the feast. Andy kept his eyes glued on the monstrous shark, not realizing that he had been holding his breath since the creature first emerged from the depths. He wasn't paying attention to the other sharks, but they had finally taken notice of the two divers in their territory. They began to swim closer and closer to the cage, their circles tightening up as they evaluated the metal cage with their cold, dead eyes. Just as their presence registered with Andy, he realized why Derrick was poking him in the ribs. The cage rattled violently as an aggressive male shark rammed his snout into the cage. Derrick dropped the camera as he reached out to brace the cage as if that would help keep the steel bars together. Andy looked around as the *Carcharodons* buzzed around them, amped up on the smell of blood and the presence of the CCGS *Heart's Content* which sent electrical impulses to their brain, tricking them into thinking the coast guard ship was a predator.

Once the first shark bumped the cage and swam away unharmed, the others quickly lost their fear of Andy and Derrick. Andy ducked as an open set of jaws raced towards him, a hellish darkness set in between rows of jagged, razor-sharp teeth. The shark tried to take a bite of the steel; its jaw gaped open right in front of Andy. The inch-thick bars were the only obstacle between Andy and his demise. He found his muscles glued to his skeleton. Frozen in place, his heart stopped beating and his stomach twisted dreadfully as he stared into the blackness that awaited him. He closed his eyes as he heard the metal clang. Another shark smashed the side of the cage with his tale. The force was enough to send Andy toppling over into Derrick, and the two men were pinned against the far side of the cage. Andy looked up at the cable and winch, praying that someone would notice the peril they were in, but the cage swayed side to side. He sensed the vibrations from the metal cable groaning against the strain. With every attack from below, the only thing keeping Andy and Derrick from plummeting to their doom threatened to collapse. The booming, metallic twangs pierced into Andy's eardrum as the cage rocked violently from an unseen force below. One of the guide lines snapped on the cage sending out a shrill metallic roar as the cage dropped at an odd angle, pinning Andy on top of Derrick.

Andy looked on in bewilderment as the sharks seemingly disappeared into thin air. The twenty-five foot female released her death grip on the whale's hide and did one semi-circle near the humpback before fleeing into the distance. Andy could hear his heartbeat thumping inside his chest, his pulse thumping aggressively in his wrist. There was an eerie silence in the ocean. The humpbacks shredded remains swayed back and forth softly with the ocean current, the last of the mammal's blood long expelled from its ravaged body.

The mechanic roar of the boats wench finally rumbled to life, but the cage seemed to be stuck in place, the three remaining guide lines barely hanging on anymore. Something hit Andy in the back. His heart leapt out of his mouth as he spun around to see the camera floating carelessly inside the cage. A flood of relief washed over his body. He found himself laughing as a flood of bubbles escaped from under his mask. He reached out to nab the camera when he saw a soft white glow raising from the murky darkness below. At first it seemed small, but it continued to grow. The soft white glow was just a blob of light, but

Andy could tell whatever created the glow was massive. He felt the cage bounce and rattle as the tension on the cable began to raise the cage. He looked up just in time to hear the powerful snap as the remaining guide lines tore from the cage. Suddenly he found himself motionless. Time stood still for a moment before the cage began its rapid descent into the briny depths.

CHAPTER TWENTY

Arctic Ocean

The smallest ocean in the world, the Arctic Ocean, is also the shallowest of the world's oceans. It is situated in the north polar region and is mostly surrounded by Eurasia and North America. The ocean has limited access to the rest of the world and has its own complex system of water flows. Because the density of seawater increases as it nears the freezing point, it tends to sink. While the top layer of water is covered with sea ice, the relatively warm ocean water keeps the temperature moderate. This is the big reason why the Arctic does not experience the extreme weather conditions seen in the Antarctic continent.

The strongest impact of global warming can be seen in the Arctic. Some of the oldest and thickest ice in the waters just north of Greenland, which remain frozen year round, have begun to break up. The sea off the north coast of Greenland had remained frozen since the last ice age, but warm winds and abnormal heat waves have caused the ice to retreat further away from the coast. The arctic ice pack is a large section of sea ice that covers most of the Arctic ocean. This ice melts in the spring and summer but returns in the fall and winter in a continuous cycle. Global warming is giving the spring and summer months an advantage. Each year less and less of the Arctic basin sea ice remains

Darwinism can be summed up by one picture. That picture that shows how man evolved from an ape. Everyone has, at one point in their life, seen the poster somewhere. The theory states that species who have the strongest ability to compete for food, survive its environment, and reproduce successfully will continue. Those species that are unable to adapt will be weaned out by natural selection. It has been often described as the survival of the fittest. This form of evolution is the most commonly accepted theory for new species. Another theory that was developed by Dutch geneticist Hugo de Vries added another layer to Charles Darwin's widely accepted theory. The mutation theory suggested that not all species evolved through the slow accumulation of variation over vast periods of time. Mutation theory suggested that some species were brought to life by rapid transformations, often caused by an extreme change of environment for members of a species that have been separated from the majority of its own kind. The one thing that both theories have in common is that these evolutionary changes are beneficial for the new species to survive. The problem with mutation theory that we chose to ignore is that sometime these mutations create dangerous monstrosities, an abomination within an already deadly species.

Carcharodon carcharias is not normally found in the Arctic ocean, the waters much too cool and the food source unable to sustain a thriving subspecies of the great white shark. Most of the great white sharks who have ever ventured into the unforgiving Arctic Ocean quickly leave. However, a *Carcharodon carcharias* birthed into the environment managed to survive even though its mother died shortly after its birth. Bergmann's law dictated that the shark grow exponentially in order to generate enough heat to survive. The cold waters were relentless, forcing the shark to grow far beyond its species' capabilities. The great white shark was already forty-two feet long and was still growing. It weighed over seven-thousand kilograms, its powerful muscles able to generate more force than any creature in the ocean. Its jaw was the size of a small truck, lined with six rows of four-inch razor-sharp teeth that looked more like steak knives sticking out of its pink gums. Its gnarled mouth contained over four hundred of these triangle-shaped, flesh-tearing tools in its unhinged jaw. Able to exert a bite force just over twenty-thousand newtons, it could quickly disable its prey with one devastating bite. The predator had never seen the light of day, keeping itself hidden underneath the ice floes. It feasted on stray walruses and smaller whales who dared venture beneath the ice floes with it. The grey pigmentation of its skin was no longer necessary and another genetic mutation took place, causing albinism over a few years. Its hide was as pristine and white as the ice above it. As with all creatures affected by albinism, its eyes had no pigmentation. Every vein that ran to the creature's eye turned the white iris blood red.

Now, over the years as the ice retreated, covering less and less of the ocean, the apex predator was quickly running out of places to hide. A strong magnetic force from deep within the earth had called the solitary shark back to its ancestors' breeding ground just off the shores of Newfoundland. The maturing albino *Carcharodon carcharias* could feel the urge to mate overcoming all of its basic needs except for one other. It had followed the frigid melting ice down the Labrador Current and all the way to the southern coast of Newfoundland where it waited patiently for the sun to set. Its powerful sense of smell picked up the scent of a large whale. Its ampullae of Lorenzini could sense that the creature's heart was no longer beating. Not wanting to miss out on an easy meal, the gigantic *Carcharodon carcharias* began its ascent towards the surface. It needed to feed.

CHAPTER TWENTY-ONE

Shark Cage
Atlantic Ocean
Cliffs of the Grand Banks

The pressure began to build in Andy's ear as the cage dragged him down into the blackness. The light blue waters quickly changed to a deeper shade of blue then purple. His mind raced faster than the steel casket that was bringing him to his final resting place. Derrick's arm bumped his head, reminding Andy that at least he wouldn't have to die alone. The white light continued to glow as the cage plummeted past the ghostly figure that was now hovering above them like a malevolent spirit. Andy was in agony from the pressure building inside of his cranium. If he didn't stop his descent, his skull would implode at any moment. His brain was being forced at from all angles. His eyes felt like they were about to erupt out of their sockets. Suddenly a force reached out and caught Andy by the arm. He watched the steel cage continue its descent until it dissolved away into the shadows.

Derrick had opened the top of the cage, and the two men floated next to each other encased in darkness, unsure of which way was up or down. Derrick shook Andy until their eyes locked. He stared into his friend's eyes full of panic. The left eye was completely blood shot leaving only traces of the white iris behind, the pressure bursting a vessel. Andy knew they were far too deep. They had to act before the crushing force surrounding them was too much to bear. Kicking his legs, Andy and Derrick both started to move in the direction they prayed was up. Andy started to claw his hands at the water above his head, trying to grasp the water and pull himself towards the surface faster. Soon the purple water faded, and the deep blue water signalled that they were on the right path. Every muscle in Andy's body began to cramp, his legs as useless as two lead weights, his quad strings growing tighter with every kick. His shoulder and back muscles were tense, acute pain shooting up and down his arms, the pain threatening to shut them down. A knot developed in his neck, forcing him to look down. Shadows seemed to be churning in the blackness beneath, preparing to reach out and drag him back down at any moment.

The deep blue slowly turned a softer shade, the glimmers of sunlight invigorating him enough to keep his arms and legs churning. Andy broke the surface and ripped his mask off, sucking in enough fresh air to fill his lungs. The orange sun beat down on him, thawing his chilled soul.

"Get out of the water!" frantic voices screamed from behind Andy.

A loud splash startled Andy, his heart sank to the bottom of the ocean expecting a set of jaws beside him. He was relieved to find Derrick had breached the surface. "Let's get out of here." Andy began to laugh uncontrollably after cheating death. Derrick pulled off his mask and joined in and nearly choked on a mouthful of salt water as a wave splashed over both men, the briny water stinging Andy's eyes.

"Hurry up!"

"Come on, swim!"

"Move, you fools!"

Andy turned towards the sound of the delirious shouting. The CCGS *Heart's Content* towered over them, its sleek black hull about thirty metres away. Andy raised his arms and waved before giving a thumbs up, signalling that he was okay. He couldn't pick out the distraught faces or agitated voices from the distance, the sun burning brightly behind them, obscuring their features.

"Holy fuck!" Derrick roared, his arms and legs thrashing in the water as he broke off, swimming towards the coast guard ship.

"You have to move, Andy!"

"Don't look, just swim!"

"Move, you fucking idiot!"

Andy turned left towards where the humpback whale should have been to find that it had disappeared. He kept turning around, expecting to see that the great white sharks had returned, but his mouth hung open when he saw it. A five-foot, pure white dorsal fin sliced through the water leaving a three-foot wake behind it. Andy froze in place, not from exhaustion but from the terrifying realization of why the other sharks had fled. A predator much larger had staked its claim over these waters and was now patrolling the area for intruders. The dorsal fin slowly slid underneath the waves. Andy watched as the impossibly large albino *Carcharodon* slipped beneath the surface, its ghastly white glow more terrifying than any shadow that had ever crept up from below. Andy turned and started to swim towards the CCGS *Heart's Content*, the ungodly glow circling beneath him.

CCGS Heart's Content
Atlantic Ocean
Cliffs of the Grand Banks

Kate didn't believe her eyes. The albino abomination's mammoth jaws had exploded from beneath the humpback whales carcass, the sheer force that the shark had generated sent the creature soaring above the blue waters. The forty-two foot anomaly hovered out of the water for what seemed like an eternity before gravity reached out and brought it back down. The alabaster shark landed on top of the remaining whale, and the two creatures disappeared underneath an enormous upsurge of salt water. When the vast aftershock of waves finally dissipated, the two giant creatures had vanished from view as if they had never existed.

Then she saw the dorsal fin grow from beneath the waves. The ghost-white hide of the creature glowed brightly beneath the water. The creature was headed straight towards Andy and Derrick as people urged them to swim towards the boat. Now the ethereal glow circled beneath the two men, their arms and legs thrashing wildly through the rough seas straight towards them. "Oh, my god!" Kate stammered as she realized that the creature was getting ready to strike. She rushed down the metal stairs, skipping two at a time, and dashed towards the rail of the ship. "Lewis, you have to get them out of the water now."

Captain Lewis Park turned around; his soft blue eyes filled with terror as he acknowledged his ex-girlfriend. "Grab a life ring and throw it in." Lewis pointed towards the white and red flotation device along the sterling silver wall. He had already tossed one of the rings overboard, but there wouldn't be enough time for Lewis to rescue both men. Everyone else fled in panic, cowering at the sight of the monstrosity that was nearly the same size as their boat.

Kate grabbed the rubber ring and dragged it towards the rail, the length of rope tied off to a hitch on the wall made it much heavier than it looked. She struggled with it. Lewis rushed over and grasped hold of it, dragging Kate across the deck with it.

"Let go!" Lewis barked as they reached the metal railing.

Kate let go just before Lewis hoisted the life ring up to his chest and flung it overboard. Kate couldn't stop the forward momentum that Lewis had generated, and she tumbled over her own feet trying to stop on the slippery deck. Her face narrowly missed the rail as her hand darted out in front of her to brace her own fall. Her fingers bent backwards at an awkward angle, and she felt the calcium in her knuckles pop as they twisted back towards her wrist. Lewis gently placed his hand on her shoulder and helped her up. "Thanks." Kate's voice was faint. The pain welled up in her hands instantly.

The rope hanging over the rail tightened suddenly. Kate looked over and saw Andy had raced past Derrick, reaching the life ring first. The smile that crossed her face quickly fled. A sense of dread curled the corner of her lips as she watched the white blur grow larger as the alabaster great white swept underneath both men, disappearing beneath the *Heart's Content*. Kate tried with all of her might to pull Andy up, straining with every last ounce of strength to move him. Andy reached his arms over his head, grasping at the rope and pulled himself up the side of the hull hand over fist.

"I need your help," Lewis urged. The strain of pulling Derrick up had turned his face bright red. The veins in his taut neck stuck out like mighty rivers running over rocky mountains.

"What about Andy?" Kate braced herself against the side of the rail with her feet, trying desperately to get some leverage.

"He'll be on board before Derrick," Lewis barked at Kate in a voice he ordinarily reserved for their fierce arguments when they dated. "We need help over here!" Lewis cried out in vain. The rest of the crew were scrambling around, much too frightened to approach the edge of the ship.

Ellen appeared seemingly out of thin air Kate noticed her hands had clasped hold of the cable. Ellen's hand lay just over the top of where Lewis had grabbed. The bright glow appeared once more. This time the shark's form was clear enough that Kate could pick out the different fins on its body. The *Carcharodon* turned its snout directly towards Derrick. The shark could sense the panicked flailing of his limbs as he thrashed wildly in the water. The five-foot dorsal fin emerged from the water for a moment then dove straight down twenty metres before reaching its intended prey. Cries of agony and distress could be heard from behind the chaos, people too afraid to help but unable to turn away from the nightmarish scene. A wave left from the wake of the shark's ascent caught Derrick in its flow, sending his body crashing into the hull of the boat. The loud bang as his back smashed into the boat made Kate cringe, the sound echoing up the hull.

"Hold on, Derrick!" Ellen called out in between staggered breaths.

Kate finally let go of Andy's rope and got behind Ellen, hauling the rope with all of her might. They watched as Derrick slowly began to rise out of the water. Everyone breathed heavy, grunting loudly as they grappled with the dead weight. Derrick's body dangled precariously three feet over the surface when Kate noticed the white-hot glow directly below him.

Andy's hand reached up and clasped the rail. His forearm muscles looked like they were about to burst out of his skin. "Andy!" Kate cried out as she watched him pull himself over the rail. Andy toppled over the top and fell hard onto the deck, his chest heaving up and down from exhaustion. "You're okay," she said. Andy laid on his back, resting his hand over his stomach.

Kate kept tugging on the cable. The three of them were finally appearing to generate some actual progress getting Derrick out of the water when the white glow rushed towards the surface, a black hole opening in the center. Before anyone was able to react, the rope slackened, and they all tumbled backwards, falling over each other. A giant spray of foamy white water swept over the deck as the albino shark breached the surface, soaking Kate to the bone. She looked up as the giant shark rose above them, its belly, as pure white as fresh fallen snow, blocking out the sun. Kate shuddered and closed her eyes, waiting for the immense body to crush them as it fell back down. After what seemed like an eternity, she heard a giant splash as the shark fell backwards into the water. Giant waves rocked the boat violently, a force generated by the seven-thousand kilograms slamming back into the ocean.

A loud scream forced Kate to open her eyes. Andy's cries of anguish jolted her senses, forcing her to gasp at the gruesome sight. Derrick's arms were tangled around the metal rails, grasping on for dear life. The blood had drained from his face, his eyes stuck open in a permanent shocked expression. His lips quivered as he struggled to speak, scarlet blood trickling from his mouth. Bubbles formed from the corner of his jaws as he tried to breathe. Derrick's upper torso ended just above the hips, the lower half of his stomach spewing blood and entrails as his innards fell into the water below. Kate wanted to throw up as she listened to the soft contents of his stomach plopping against the surface below.

Ellen choked back a cry, the deep sobs catching in her throat nearly cutting off her supply of oxygen. Andy was the first to his feet. He ran over to comfort his friend in a vain attempt. "You're going to be alright." His voice trembled. Derrick stared at him with a sorrowful expression on his face, not accepting what Andy had claimed. Andy tried to haul Derrick onto the deck, a frivolous endeavor to prevent his friend from becoming shark food. Andy slipped in the blood that had spilled over onto the deck, his face falling inches away from Derrick's severed torso.

"Get away from me." The words sputtered out of Derrick's throat in a gargled, wet sob, the blood blocking the words from escaping his mouth.

"I need help." Andy struggled to move his friend; his body was pinned against the rail. The rope from the life raft had wrapped around his mangled body and restrained him against the cold metal. Ellen and Lewis rushed forward, nearly pushing Kate out of the way as she tried to help Andy with the rope.

"Move," Lewis demanded, pulling a large knife out of the sheath attached to his black leather belt. The sunlight reflected the blazing sun along the razor-sharp edge. The blade looked sharp enough to split atoms. Lewis grabbed a length of rope and sliced through the rope with ease. The binds holding Derrick in place loosened enough for Andy and Kate to lower his body onto the deck of the *Heart's Content*. The last of his life blood flooded out of his body. His spine had been snapped clean in half from the vicious bite. All the colour had drained from Derrick's face. His eyes remained open, the terror bulging them outwards as if they were about to pop out of the sockets as any moment.

"Thanks," Andy mumbled as he knelt over his friend's corpse. Lewis patted Andy on the shoulder, unable to find any comforting words.

Kate reached out and pulled Andy into her body, his face buried into her neck. Warm tears fell from his cheek and formed a puddle in the nape of her neck. Andy's body convulsed as he began to weep passionately. Kate ran her fingers through his hair as he let out a surge of emotions and frustration. Ellen and Lewis began to untangle the rest of the rope from Derrick as Andy grieved the loss of his friend. Kate watched Ellen step into a coil of black rope that they had thrown overboard for Andy, the life ring still floating on the surface of the ocean.

"Ellen!" Kate began to scream, but a loud twang cut her off. The rope went taut, and the coil tightened around her ankle. A loud metallic pop echoed through the air as the hook holding the rope burst off the wall. Ellen's eyes grew wide and her jaw dropped as the back of her head slammed into the rail with a loud crack. Then, as the rope continued to tug at her leg, yanking her up and over as her body flipped over the rail. Her limbs flailing around as the impact knocked her unconscious. Her body disappeared over the side and plunged down into the ocean, the length of rope dragging her into the dismal abyss.

Lewis leapt over the side of the ship after her, the knife clenched in his jaws.

Open Water
Atlantic Ocean
Cliffs of the Grand Banks

The water frothed up, sending out ripples from the spot where Ellen had plummeted into the cold waters. As Lewis dove headfirst into the disturbed water, he saw Ellen reaching up towards the surface, almost as if she was reaching out for his hand. The salt water stung Lewis's eyes as he broke through the rough ocean. He forced himself to keep them open. He wouldn't risk losing sight of Ellen. Her jet black hair blended in with the ink-black waters, exaggerating the brightness of lipstick and bronzed skin. The white glow of the shark was rapidly drawing away at and odd angle. Lewis couldn't tell if the shark was descending or going straight. All he knew was Ellen was plunging deeper. Her hands fidgeted with the ropes in a frivolous attempt to loosen the constraint it had over her ankle. She was pulling away faster than Lewis could swim. His lungs began to burn as he tried to hold on long enough to reach her.

The rope pulled tighter and the force of the shark had finally taken its toll on Ellen's ankle joint. A loud pop reverberated as the ball joint tore out of the socket. All the flesh, muscle, and sinew below the rope ripped clean off. A large red cloud burst into the air. Ellen screamed out in anguish as a torrent of bubbles danced over her face. Lewis pumped his arms and legs harder. The white glow shifted direction abruptly as the aura of blood circulated throughout the salt water. Ellen's head lurched back, her dying gaze fixed on Lewis. Her arms and legs stopped moving as the cold, saline water filled her lungs and abdomen, causing her to sink down into the abyss like an anchor. Lewis started to kick his legs, recognizing that he'd never be able to reach her before he would be obliged to accompany her at the bottom of the ocean.

Lewis looked down one last time, wishing that he hadn't. The albino shark barreled towards Ellen faster than anything Lewis had ever seen in the ocean. It's massive, snarled-tooth jaws snapped open wide enough to swallow her whole. As the alabaster *Carcharodon* clamped its jaws shut, the razor-sharp teeth severed Ellen's outstretched arm. A detonation of blood erupted like a blossoming flower, draining over the shark as it rushed past.

Lewis turned his head towards the surface and swam with all of his might, a trickle of light from the blazing sun above him. He wouldn't dare look down, knowing that if he saw the *Carcharodon carcharias* coming for him, he would freeze in place. The shadow of the CCGS *Heart's Content* loomed over the surface, close enough now that he was able to distinguish the mast and cabins resting on the deck.

Lewis embraced the warm air kissing his hand as it breached the surface for a brief moment, like a lover's tender embrace. The sensation of swimming in quicksand took over, as an unseen force tugged at his legs, holding him in place. The water began to flow like a violent river, the force pressing in on him from all around. The warmth of the sun was snatched away without warning as he began to sink deeper into a dark void racing up from beneath him. A force stronger than a freight train erupted beneath him. The sun disappeared in an instant and everything was cast into complete darkness. Gravity seemed to have no effect over him, he felt like his body was soaring through the air. Lewis hung weightless in a void of pitch black. A putrid, sour stench overwhelmed him. The smell of decomposing fish and flesh churned all around him. Lewis realized that the alabaster shark had swallowed him whole, and now he was left alive in this hellish nightmare. He reached to his pistol, pulling back the safety, and decided he wasn't going down without a fight. He fired twice, the booming sound echoing off the shark's thick hide. As the muzzle flashed, his own grotesque casket was brought to life, like the flash on a camera taking pictures in the dark. Hunks of Ellen's flesh caught in the jagged, four-inch teeth lined the creature's death trap.

A surge of water as the shark opened its mouth dragged Lewis down. Murky blue water sparkled brightly against the pure darkness enveloping him for a moment. He tried to swim towards the opening, his lungs burning with ex-cruciating pain. His body was now drained of the energy required to fight the current pulling him deeper into the shark's stomach. The light disappeared in a violent snap. A colossal force snapped his spine clean through as the razor-sharp teeth clamped together, severing Lewis Park in half.

CHAPTER TWENTY-TWO

CCGS Heart's Content
Atlantic Ocean
Cliffs of the Grand Banks

Andy watched in horror as the ethereal glow rushed towards the CCGS *Heart's Content*, the snow-white dorsal fin slicing through the three-foot waves. The Carcharodon swam with fierce grace. Her body moved with ease through the waters as her powerful torso and caudal fin pumped savagely. The shark closed the distance quickly, moving through the rough seas at over forty knots. Not one of the crew knew what to do; the boat was laying directly in the path of the monstrous great white shark. A giant cloud of black soot filled the air. The ship's engine rumbled much too late. Andy could smell the heavy, choking fumes sputtering from below deck as someone tried to force the *Heart's Content* to move before its time. Andy could feel the vibrations shuttering through the hull.

"Grab on to something sturdy." Andy turned towards Kate. The brilliant glow of the sun caught in her hair, and for a moment Andy wondered if he had already died and was now looking up at an angel.

"What?" Kate asked confused, her body trembling with fear. Her bottom lip quivered as she spoke.

Andy grabbed Kate around the waist, pulling her towards the center of the boat by her belt. They reached the rail of a staircase leading up to the helm. Kate tried to run up the stairs but Andy held her tight. "Wait here and hold on." Racing up the stairs, bounding up them two at a time, Andy moved towards the main deck. He burst through the door and looked around at the terrified faces buried into their computer screens. Their faces were illuminated by a pale green from the monitors. "Where are the keys to the submersible?" No one answered him. Everyone was waiting for the boat to move. Andy knew they couldn't outrun the giant shark in this giant ship, but he may out-maneuver the creature. He had to stay on top of his game, keep the creature guessing his next move. "Hey can someone..."

SMASH

The albino *Carcharodon carcharias* rammed the stern of the CCGS *Heart's Content*, sending a vicious shock wave throughout the ship. Andy fell face-first into some computer equipment as the ship whirled hard to starboard. The vibrations of the engines had enraged the great white. Now they sputtered and choked. The whole room filled with the loud bangs of equipment crashing to the ground, glass shattering, and the anguished screams of the crew. A loud metallic groan wailed from the engine room as the gears struggled to keep turning.

"Turn the engines off!" Andy called out as he climbed back to his feet. "You need to turn them off now!" He barked, but no one listened.

"The shark is attracted to the vibrations from them. If you don't turn them off, it will keep attacking us," Kate stated calmly. There was a bright red gash across her forehead spilling crimson blood over her face.

Andy rushed to her side. "Are you okay?"

"Turn off those fucking engines!" Kate screeched, her voice shrill and full of anger.

BOOM

An explosion rattled the entire ship as the engine blew up, sending a shock wave through the ocean. Every computer screen that hadn't been destroyed during the impact a moment ago now lost power. The red emergency lights flicked on overhead as a loud siren rang overhead. The acidic scent of fire and fuel soured the air. Andy started sweating as a wave of heat from the fire below deck washed over him.

"Close off the engine room," a woman spoke into a walkie-talkie. "Flood the ballast to douse the fire."

"It's swimming away!" A sailor called out gleefully, his finger pointing out the window.

Andy walked over and watched in disbelief, the dorsal fin slicing through the waves with ease. Kate's warm breath sent a riptide of goosebumps through his body. Her lips inches away from his neck as she leaned against him. Her body went limp, her weight crashing down over him as she collapsed into him. "Kate." Andy caught her underneath the arm just before she slammed face-first in front of him. He eased her down, the blood flowing from the deep gash on her forehead that ran into her hairline and disappeared beneath a wet clump of her hair. He placed his finger on her neck, and a flood of relief washed over him as he found her faint heartbeat still pulsating in her neck. "Wake up, Kate." Andy shook her gently, her chest rising and falling slowly as she breathed.

"We are taking on water," a static filled voiced came in over the walkie-talkie.

"It's circling us."

"It can sense we are sinking."

"What do we do, Ali?" Her crew looked to their supervisor.

A loud metallic groan echoed beneath them as an incessant torrent of water threatened to sink the *Heart's Content*. It crippled the ship. They were a sitting duck in the middle of the Atlantic Ocean. The biggest *Carcharodon carcharias* ever encircled them, waiting for its prey to enter the water with it. Andy stared down at Kate's ghastly pale face; the blood spattered over her gorgeous eyes.

"Get the life rafts in the water," Ali ordered.

"That thing will pick them off. You won't stand a chance out there with it waiting to strike," Andy objected.

"We will sink before help can reach us and there's no fucking way, I'm getting into the water with it," Ali argued, ignoring Andy's warning.

"Call for help and you may get off this ship alive." Andy stood up and turned his back to Ali, looking out of the window as the dorsal fin patrolled the water just one-hundred metres away.

"Are you deaf or just plain stupid? We won't stay afloat long enough." Frustration ripped through Ali's throat, each word spitting out in anger. "Unless you have some plan, I'm lowering those life boats."

"You're right, you do have to get those life boats lowered but not yet." Andy continued to marvel at the snow-white dorsal fin as it cut the waves in half.

"I'm not waiting for that thing to get closer. We need to go now while it's still far enough away. We may have a chance if it doesn't catch us leaving."

"That shark will sense the exact second you place anything into its domain. Its radar senses work much better than what you have on this ship." Andy let out a chuckle. "I'll grab its attention and you can make a run for it once the shark is entertained. I'll lead it away."

"How do you plan to do that, cowboy?" Ali mocked him.

Andy spun around to look at Kate. "Get me the keys for that submersible."

CHAPTER TWENTY-THREE

CCGS Heart's Content
Atlantic Ocean
Deep Sea Submersible Pegasus

Andy climbed into the cockpit of the two-man deep-submergence vehicle *Pegasus*. The inside of the cockpit reminded him of something he would have seen on *Lost in Space*. There were over-sized buttons, dials, toggles, and an LCD display screen that emitted a pale green glow. A musty smell from beneath the seat suggested that it had been a while since anyone had done maintenance on the deep-submergence vehicle. Andy cursed under his breath at the crew for neglecting the extraordinarily advanced technology in favor of their daily routine. The swathes of stainless steel ran into the polished black floor, the light gleaming along the outline of the component of his high-tech dashboard.

Clink clink clink clink

A metallic squeal rang out overhead as the chains lowing the *Pegasus* struggled against the rust and grime buildup, threatening to break and send Andy careening down into the deep blue ocean. As each link passed through the pulley system, the sub bounced, held in place for a moment before dropping back down until the next stoppage. Andy powered up the twin-turbo engine. The power of the engine surging throughout the entire cockpit sent jitters through his whole body. The submarine was only designed to go thirty knots, so he couldn't outrun the albino *Carcharodon carcharias*. His best chance of survival would be to outmaneuver the speedy shark. When the sub finally reached the water, the waves lapped over the acrylic glass dome, the crystal clear sky slowly fading into the murky mess surrounding the boat. The CCGS *Heart's Content* damaged engines were spewing oil into the Atlantic Ocean. The remains of the humpback water floated through the water like a heavy haze. Andy looked at the sonar screen and immediately picked up two giant blips. The behemoth shark had closed the gap to just fifty metres now. The movement of the dominant great white was too much for the radar to keep track of. A brief delay in reporting the creature's position could prove catastrophic. "Come on." Andy slapped the screen with an open palm, hoping that would solve his dilemma.

He turned the bright white lights on. His heart dropped in his chest as he couldn't see much more than ten metres ahead of him, enclosed by the carnage next to the ship. He ran his fingers along the toggles until he found the release switch for the chains. The submarine floated freely in the water, bobbing up and down in the waves. The bright blue sky overhead was tarnished with tall pillars of jet black smoke from the *Heart's Content's* burning engines. The white dorsal fin changed directions now, cutting its tight circle in half to investigate the electronic impulses sent out by the *Pegasus*. His natural instincts took over. The desire for self-preservation pushed the throttle forward. Andy sent the sub into a sharp spiral downwards, trying to find an escape from the thick slurry of blood and oil that clouded his vision. Every passing moment was sheer agony. Dark shadows followed him at every turn, waiting to reach out and take hold of the sub.

The light finally broke into the ink-black waters of the depths as the *Pegasus* sped down the shelf of the Grand Banks two-hundred metres below the surface. Now Andy was able see forty metres ahead of him, the light seeping into the blackness ahead of him. Checking his radar, Andy wasn't shocked to find that the great white had closed the gap to twenty metres and was now following the *Pegasus* from behind. Andy craned his neck and looked over his shoulder through the crystal-clear glass. The white glow shined like a bright light at the end of a dark hallway. "Fuck," Andy said to himself as he pushed the deep-submergence vehicle further down into deep waters, not wanting to afford the *Carcharodon* the opportunity to strike from below. With the ability to gather the force of a locomotive, it would certainly prove to be a devastating blow. Even the tiniest puncture to the acrylic dome would allow the pressures of the deep into the cockpit, crushing Andy's skull like Gallagher hitting a watermelon with that hammer. The *Pegasus* soared through the abyss, the white hot glow trailing his every move as Andy deviated left and right. He was desperately trying to keep his pursuer off guard long enough for the crew of the *Heart's Content* to make it to safety.

As Andy pushed deeper into the blackness, white particles drifted past the clear glass, giving him the illusion he was flying through space. The tiny white dots reflected the sub's own light back at it, like stars in the Milky Way. "This is insane," Andy laughed as the alien form behind him kept pace with him through every twist and turn. The ocean floor came into view, the rocky bottom covered in barnacles and underwater vegetation that hid hundreds of species from predators. Andy maneuvered the *Pegasus* as closely as possible, hoping that would deter the giant beast stalking him. The pure white belly of the alabaster shark passed over head. Andy banked sharply to port, narrowly avoiding a giant outcrop of rocks as he twisted the controls of the submarine. He found himself upside down, the ocean floor now a ceiling. Andy was trapped in a confined space with the evil monstrosity. Its bloodshot eyes pierced through the light beam, following it to the *Pegasus*. Flops of sweat formed in an instant on his forehead. A wave of heat rushed through his body as the weight of claustrophobia washed over him. Andy cringed as a crushing sound echoed all around him. The cockpit was being squeezed shut. His breathing came in short gasps and fear's fingers dug in between his ribs, holding his chest in place with anxiety. Andy began to lose consciousness as the jaws gaped open and jutted forward. Rows of jagged, razor-sharp teeth sprang out past the shark's snout as its jaws unhinged. Andy stared into the darkest void; a blackness so intense there was no escape from its reach.

Life Rafts
Atlantic Ocean

Ali cradled Kate's head in between her thighs, the blood from the deep gash on her forehead soaking into her pants. Ali felt the sticky fluid against her skin, the heat fusing a bond between the fabric of her pants and her legs, using the blood as a bonding agent. "Sheldon can you locate land yet?" Ali asked, her back pinned against the rubber side of the life raft.

"Not yet," Sheldon answered in a disheartened voice as he leaned on the edge of the raft.

The yellow life raft had a built-in motor. Melvin had intuitively taken command of it when the four of them first got in the raft. The roaring buzz of four other engines could be heard as the twenty surviving crew members raced towards shore. Each one of the rubber bottoms slapped off the water as they hopped over the waves. There was enough room in their raft to fit all twenty people, but they came to an agreement to take five life rafts. If that shark decided to pick off one of the boats at least the rest would still make to land. "We will find it soon, I can tell," Melvin said excitedly.

"I can't believe this is actually happening," Ali whispered to Kate, looking down at the extensive wound. Ali tilted her head back to scan the horizon, expecting to see the five-foot, pure white dorsal fin streaming towards one of the life rafts at any moment.

"The worst part'all this is over now," Melvin reassured her. "Just put your faith in the lord. He'll lead us home yet."

"How can you be so sure?" Sheldon asked pessimistically.

"We're still here, ain't we?" Melvin pointed his finger over Ali's shoulder. "Well ain't that a sight for sore eyes. I've never been so happy spotting land."

Ali looked over her shoulder as the land began to come into plain view, poking out through a thin veil of mist from about two kilometres away. The green trees blended together, making the island appear like one giant shrub sticking out of the water. "We are still here." Ali gave Kate's shoulder a tight squeeze. She used her index finger to find a strong pulse pumping in Kate's neck, her jugular throbbing underneath her skin.

"Where are we?" Kate's voice was muddled by confusion. Her eyelids batted open and closed as she struggled to block the sun out of her eyes while trying to search for a prominent landmark.

"We are safe now," Melvin reassured her.

"We are almost back to land," Ali added.

Kate looked around the raft, her face wrought with anguish. Her lips writhed into an expression of torment. "Where is Andy?"

There was nothing but the rumble of the outboard motors as the five life rafts raced across the water. Everyone was rendered speechless. Ali sought to figure out something to say other than *I don't know*. She didn't want to upset the poor girl in her lap; she had been through enough already. Ali watched as Kate's chest rose and collapsed back into itself more rapidly now. The realization of what she had just witnessed began to come back to her. "Andy took the sub and led that demonic abomination away long enough for us to get to land."

"He'll be right behind us," Melvin chimed in. A wave rocked the boat, and everyone lost their balance except Melvin. His sea legs were much stronger than everyone else. His years on the water gave him a strength far beyond years of lifting weights could have. With practiced ease, Melvin set the raft back on course before the ocean had a chance to claim another soul.

"Would you look at that," Sheldon whined, his chin hitting his chest in defeat. "So much for taking separate rafts. They're enough of those things out there now that we are completely screwed." He pounded his fist against the raft and started to bawl.

Cliff of the Grand Banks
Atlantic Ocean
Deep-Submergence Vehicle Pegasus

Andy awoke, his body shivering from the extreme cold. His chest hurt from the savage beating of his heart. Twisted knots in his intestines forced stomach acid back up his esophagus. He choked on the burning bile on the back of his tongue. He rubbed his eyes, trying to make sense of where he was. His skull weighed down like it was full of rocks. A dark cloud hung over him. A groggy sensation combined with sharp jolts of pain firing from every synapse in his body clouded his thoughts. It was hard to fathom what he was looking at. Several teeth had punctured the glass dome of the *Pegasus*. Two inches of razor-sharp teeth had broken through but remained lodged in the acrylic glass dome. The long, white teeth were the only things keeping the pressure of these depths out of the cockpit. The sound of water rushing past gave Andy the illusion that he was stuck in a river, but he knew that he had fallen to rest on the ocean floor far below the Grand Banks. Red warning lights flicked across the screen displaying various system failures, the dull glow reflecting off the acrylic dome.

Life Support Failure
Heat Pump Failure
Engine One Failure
Engine Two Malfunction
Navigation System Failure
Buoyancy Balance Failure
Pressurization System Stable
Light System Off

"Goddammit." Andy smacked the monitor in front of him. "Give me one piece of positive news." He was losing consciousness as the carbon monoxide burned into his lungs, and he was starting to become light headed as the oxygen level plummeted. He searched under his seat, his fingers discovering the rubber mask. He pulled out the regulator that was attached to a pony tank. In a swift motion, he yanked the elastic strap over his head. Instinct told him to rotate the handle to the right. Fresh oxygen flowed into his mask and he thankfully sucked in a mouthful of air. After a long and deliberate deep breath, Andy no longer suffered from the ill effects of the carbon monoxide, the poisonous gas leaving his body. He pressed random buttons on the keyboard, hoping that some miracle might take place. He let his fingers dance across the keys, not really knowing what he was expecting to happen. Then he noticed it, a diagnostic image of *Pegasus*. Almost all the different systems of the deep-submergence vehicle were coloured red except for one engine that was a hope-bringing yellow. It was just as bright as the sun, and it warmed his soul in the same way that a warm summer's day would.

Andy turned the engines off and then tried to restart them. This time the yellow changed to green and he heard the power surge through the *Pegasus*. He could feel the raw energy coursing throughout the cabin, an incessant rumble as the engines growled to life. The diagnostic display slowly began to fill with yellow as some systems came back to life.

Life Support Critical
Heat Pump Warming
Engine One Failure
Engine Two Ready
Navigation System Searching for Signal
Buoyancy Balance Steady
Pressurization System Stable
Light System Ready

A steady flow of warmth began to spill out of the vents, fighting off the glacial chill of the abyss. He analyzed the oxygen gauge on the small tank and calculated that he had about thirty minutes or so to reach the surface. Everything would be okay as long as that hellish nightmare had returned to its domain. Turning on the lights, Andy's chest burned with pain, his heart failing to beat. With his jaw hanging open, the bright white beams revealed that the creature hadn't returned to hell. Andy found himself trapped in the jaws of the Albino *Carcharodon carcharias* as it glided through the depths. He powered up the engine and tried to burst clear from the monstrous jaws of the snow white *Carcharodon*. The lights illuminated the ghast-ly insides of the demonic creature as the *Pegasus* shifted, the nose of the submarine now pointing straight down into the creature's unfathomable gullet. Andy gagged at the flecks of flesh still caught in between the creature's jaws. A swatch of fabric that had belonged to Ellen's jeans was stuck on the jagged edge of a tooth. Andy covered his face with his hand, preventing the bile from spilling out. Vomit burned his throat as it filled his mouth. He ripped off his oxygen mask just in time. Andy threw up into his own lap. The hot liquid splashed against his legs and promptly turned cold again.

Spitting out a mouthful of reddish brown slime, a bit-ter, metallic tang filled his mouth. Andy wanted to turn away from the carnage, but he needed to force his way out of the beast's mouth. The radiant light beam flickered, and the surge of the engine rattled obnoxiously as the deep-submergence vehicle began to run out of electricity. At this rate, his oxygen would last longer than the battery cell. He didn't want to die down here in the dark, waiting for the unknown to come take him. Andy pulled his mask back over his face then he peeked down at the control panel once more. Specks of spittle had spattered onto the screen. He wiped it away with the sleeve of his arm and turned off the heat pump in an effort to conserve battery power. A tear rolled down Andy's face as he flicked through the diagnostics system, unable to find a solution to his dire dilemma. He pounded his fist against his thighs in exas-peration over and over until his legs were numb, unable to take it anymore. The bones in his hands ached, and his knuckles were white as his fists clenched in anger.

"Come on, you bastard!" Andy screamed out at the top of his lungs. "Finish me." His voice reverberated off of the acrylic dome, the roar of rushing water drowning him out. Andy smashed his fist into the monitor. A spider-web pattern spread across the glass but did not break. Andy laughed breathlessly. He didn't want to suffocate, but he didn't want to be devoured whole into this demon's belly. He searched around the cabin with tear-filled eyes, his will to live silently losing the battle to the realization of his dreadful situation.

Eject

The word stood out in bright reflective tape on the side of his left leg, the lever surrounded by a plastic case.

For Emergency Use Only

"Well, this will probably be my only chance to experience how this actually functions," Andy joked, struggling to come to terms with his decision. He ran through all the scenarios in his mind; none of them involved surviving this. He reached out, lifting the case up. His fist hovered above the red lever.

Pull Out   Twist Counter-Clockwise Pull Down

He studied the directions internally, mulling over each word as if he was to be interrogated on the procedure.

"Fuck me," Andy whispered as he placed his hands on the lever. It seemed to be connected to a formidable force. He could barely pull the handle up and twist it into place. "Here goes nothing."

Andy closed his eyes and tried to picture the sun on his face one last time, but all he could see was the sinister smile of the alabaster ghoul. He didn't know what was about to happen, but Andy slammed the ejection lever down with no regrets.

CHAPTER TWENTY-FOUR

Life Rafts
Atlantic Ocean

"Quit your bellyaching, ya fool." Melvin let out a hearty chuckle. "We will be just fine. Take a gander over there,"

Sheldon raised his head up and scanned the horizon. He raised up a balled fist, slowly raising each finger. "One... Two... Three... Four... Five." He waved his hand at Melvin. "I count five dorsal fins."

Kate let out a soft whimper. "The great white sharks must have fled to the cove to get clear of that creature." Pushing herself with her elbows, she strained her neck to look into the direction of the sharks. A broad smile stretched across her face.

"What's so fucking funny?" Ali snapped at Kate. "I've had enough of this bullshit." Ali pouted like a child, letting her arms flop to her side in defeat.

"Those dorsal fins belong to orcas," Kate said, her voice full of joy. "They've come to bring us home."

"You think those things would even attempt to stop that white freak?" Sheldon said smugly. "They wouldn't stand a fucking chance," he accused Kate as if she had screwed up.

"The orca is the natural adversary of the *Carcharodon carcharias*. Millions of years of evolution will keep that creature out of this harbour. It's hard-wired to avoid these creatures." Kate's grin reached from ear to ear as the orcas circled the life rafts, guiding them towards the shore.

"You couldn't make this shit up," Melvin said as he buckled over laughing, his palm slapping off his leg as he let the fear drain out of him. "We are going to make it."

Kate nodded her head in agreement. "We are going to make it." His laughter infected Kate, and she felt a flood of relief relax her every muscle. The sharp pain in her head faded away into a dull throb that she was able to ignore, the joyous sensation overwriting the pain.

"We are going to make it?" Ali still didn't believe what was happening.

A killer whale breached just ten feet from the life raft, its sleek black skin rising into the air as it matched the speed of the boat. It continued to dive in and out of the water alongside the raft. A fine mist sprayed from the whale's blowhole every few jumps.

Cliff of the Grand Banks
Atlantic Ocean
Deep-Submergence Vehicle Pegasus Escape Pod

Andy spun out of control. The escape pod rushed towards the surface, gathering speed with every passing moment. Different shades of blue raced past his vision as the uncontrolled ascent twisted him in all directions. The hot white glow remained in the deeper blues. The sound of metal being crushed echoed through the deep water, the metallic groaning piercing into his ears. Andy was disoriented, the rapid ascent and spinning tossing him around like a wash cycle. The tension built up in his ears as the pressure changed faster than he could adjust. His stomach churned inside out, as his body rattled against the violent rocking. The seat belt tore into his shoulders, the straps threatening to break his collarbone. His neck rattled from side to side. The muscles ached as they were being stretched too far apart. The fibres and sinew ripped underneath his skin.

The escape pod burst through the ocean surface. Andy felt weightless as he soared ten feet into the air. As gravity took back over, it pulled the pod crashing down hard into the choppy blue surface. He re-entered the ocean face down, the darkness of the ocean staring back at him. He tumbled into the dashboard as the pod rolled back towards the surface. The yellow sun bobbed high above him against the blue sky. The ocean current quickly took its hold over the escape pod. Andy sensed that he was drifting aimlessly across the surface. He embraced the warmth of the sun kissing his skin like the embrace of an old lover, the sensation washing over him instantly. Andy's blood pressure dropped. The whole ordeal took its toll, sending him crashing into despair. Water lapped against the acrylic glass pod. The sound of a seagull in the distance and a strong breeze lulled Andy into a deep sleep.

The deep blue ocean surrounded the escape pod on all sides, the horizon a melting pot of blue hues. The white glow of the albino *Carcharodon carcharias* was visible underneath the escape pod, the vicious predator circling far beneath the surface. It remained hidden, waiting for the opportunity to finish its prey.

Life Rafts
Cape Race
Shipyard

The ancient wooden dock was a sight to behold, although the weathered grey boards were in desperate need of repair. The salty spray and years of negligence had withered them down to virtually nothing. The dilapidated wharf was slanted towards the depths, some boards submerged beneath the water as they descended towards the bottom. Only a few scattered boats were tied to the few remaining sturdy poles that were closer to shore, connected by colourful nylon ropes. Up on the hilltop, the Cape Race Lighthouse stood tall and proud. The white cylindrical body towered into the sky, the red top standing out against the deep blue horizon. The sight sent a shiver down Kate's spine, the image a stark reminder of the albino Carcharodon towering out of the water with its bloodied jaw. For a moment, Kate shuddered in fear, but the rocky cliffs that rose high above the ocean were a welcoming sight.

"I can't believe we made it." Ali stood up as the boat neared the dock.

"I told you we would," Melvin said matter-of-factly as he slowed the engine and let the momentum carry the life raft towards the submerged boards. "Now someone race up to that lighthouse and tell them Andy is still out there." Melvin jumped over the side, his feet splashing in the water before thudding against the dock beneath. He grabbed the guide line for the boat and held it in place, offering his hand to help people onto the wharf.

Still clouded by a deep haze, Kate was propelled forward by a surge of adrenaline flooding into her bloodstream. She leapt over the side, the cold water shocking the skin on her leg. She nearly slipped on the algae-covered boards. It was difficult traversing the treacherous dock, but her legs kept spinning until she launched herself out of the water and her shoes slapped against the weathered boards. She raced towards the rocky beach as the dock groaned beneath her. Once her foot touched solid ground, she got down on her hands and knees, kissing the soil. Euphoria washed over her. At that moment she swore she would never set foot in another boat as long as she lived. She could hear the others boats reaching the cove, their engines rumbling like thunder as the sound reverberated off the cliff faces on either side of the harbour.

Kate got back to her feet and followed the rocky path up a steep slope. Her legs shook uncontrollably underneath her, but something kept her moving. A voice in the back of her imagination reminded her of the will to get help for Andy. It also screamed at her to get as far away from the water as possible. A giant red barn crept into view at the base of the lighthouse as she crested the hill. An elderly woman knelt in a flower bed at the foot of the barn, her long silvery hair being tossed around by the breeze.

"Help."

Kate tried to yell, but the words tumbled silently out of her parched mouth. She swallowed hard, trying to draw some moisture back into her mouth. The woman looked up at the sound of rocks scuffling underneath Kate's feet, an expression of concern crossed her tanned skin. The sun had burned her skin, causing the wrinkles underneath her emerald green eyes to be that much more pronounced.

"Help." Kate managed to spew the word out, her voice shrill.

The woman jumped to her feet with a quickness you wouldn't expect from someone her age, but the terror in Kate's cry could have raised the dead. "My dear, what's the matter?" Her voice was soothing and softer than a cashmere blanket.

"My friend is out there with a monster." Kate broke down and began to whimper, her legs finally giving out as she collapsed into the ground.

"Harold, honey, you better signal for help!" she called out towards the lighthouse.

Cliffs of the Grand Banks
Atlantic Ocean
Sea King Rescue Helicopter

Blue skies raced by, the cabin shook, and the metal door frame rattled by the rotating blades while Chad gripped the edge as he peered out over the ocean. They were responding to the operator of the Cape Race Lighthouse, who had called in a distress call, giving the Coast Guard the direction of a sinking ship. The CCGS *Heart's Content* had been abandoned by all hands. Chad glanced down as they passed over the coast guard ship. The capsizing boat had rolled over onto its port side and only the underside of the hull remained above the crashing waves. Reports of a forty-foot, albino great white shark attacking the boat deterred all other ships from heading out on a rescue mission. Luckily the majority of the crew had made it to shore in the life rafts, but now the *Sea King* was searching for an electronic signal from an escape pod that had led the monstrosity away.

"We got a signal!" the pilot called out from the cockpit as he abruptly changed directions in an instant, nearly sending Chad hurtling into the ocean below. A carabiner fixed to a bar in the ceiling attached his harness kept him inside the helicopter.

"Can you give me a heads up before you do that again!" Chad yelled out, his heart racing inside his chest.

"Sorry!" the pilot called out sarcastically.

Chad shook his head as he looked out towards the horizon. The Atlantic Ocean seemed to go on forever. They could see a man, floating above the water. Chad had to look twice, rubbing his eyes to make sure his eyes weren't playing tricks on him. As the chopper approached, and as the man came into view, his features became more distinct. Sun rays beaming off the acrylic glass once the angle was right forced the pilot to adjust his approach. The sub pilot must have ejected the escape pod and was now drifting alone in the ocean. The man waved as the rumble of the *Sea King* hovered about twenty feet above the escape pod.

"I will lower the harness now," Chad informed his partner.

"Roger that."

Chad dragged the metal framed harness to the edge and gave it a tiny shove over the side. The harness fell about five feet before the slack ran out. Chad used the wench to lower it down towards the stranded man, hoping that he was healthy enough to get into the harness without assistance. A white glow formed directly beneath the acrylic escape pod from the depths. The man was frantically moving his arms and shouting, the rumble of the engine drowning out his voice. Chad quickly realized that the man wasn't trying to draw their attention to him, he was trying to warn them to get out of here.

Before Chad could react, the white hot glow opened into a dark chasm, a giant black vortex sucking in the water beneath the hovering *Sea King*. A mouth full of razor-sharp teeth exploded in a fury of destruction, swallowing the escape pod whole. The gigantic jaw continued straight up, the darkness colliding with the helicopter. Chad fell backwards as the impact sent the *Sea King* spiraling out of control. The smell of diesel and smoke filled the helicopter. Mechanical hisses and metallic groans screamed all around as the world spun into a blur. The *Sea King* smashed into the ocean with a thunderous impact. The cold ocean waters quickly filled the helicopter and pulled it down. Chad was tossed outside of the door, his mouth and nostrils filled with salt water, his body still strapped into the harness as the weight of the helicopter dragged him down with it. He tried to detach himself from the harness but couldn't reach the carabiner in time. The blue ocean quickly faded to black as he lost consciousness.

CHAPTER TWENTY-FIVE

Arctic Ocean

Joan felt her stomach turn over itself as she swam further north, the waters frigid and cold. She could still detect the scent of the large predator no matter where she went. She had followed it up through the Labrador Current and into the Arctic basin for days, hoping that she could find somewhere to give birth to her pups. She cringed, her abdominal muscles constricting as her pups writhed around inside of her belly. The time finally arrived, they were ready to come out and face the harsh waters of the freezing cold sea. Joan was exhausted. She had lost her appetite, too afraid to eat ever since she first picked up the apex predator's scent days ago. She wanted to put as much distance between them as possible, afraid that the monstrous shark would devour her newborns without blinking an eye.

This was the first time Joan found herself this far north. She kept close to the surface, basking in the warmth of the sun. The nights were almost unbearable, her muscles barely able to generate enough heat to keep her alive. Joan didn't know why, but she was following a signal buried deep beneath the ice floes. Something was drawing her there, the same signal that once brought her mother there years ago. While Joan had been birthed in the waters just above the Grand Banks, her mother found her way back to give birth three years later. A deep-rooted instinct to evolve drew Joan into this frozen hell. Now, as Joan's belly burned with the pains of child birth, she forced herself down deeper into the frigid depths of the abyss. She lost control of her stomach muscles, no longer able to hold back the pups from bursting out. Giving birth in the harsh environment would force the pups to adapt in the same way as Joan's sister had evolved.

Her stomach burned with intense pain as her body pushed the pups out. The first pup that managed to escape her womb hurt Joan the most. The other two pups passed through virtually unnoticed. Joan's body was drained from the ordeal. She floated towards the surface in a daze, leaving her children to fend for themselves. Their instinct would soon take over, allowing them to gorge on the slow moving prey drifting aimlessly along the bottom. Her pups would easily adapt to the frigid waters of the Arctic ocean because they had been born into them. Joan was not so lucky. The cold waters drained the remaining energy from her exhausted muscles. She wasn't able to keep moving forward anymore. Unable to force water through her lungs, Joan drowned. Her body sank to the ocean floor for her young to feast upon. She slowly suffocated as she suffered the razor-sharp teeth ripping into her flesh.

CHAPTER TWENTY-SIX

St. John's International Airport
Terminal
St. John's, NL

Kate sat in a hard plastic chair, her feet folded up beneath her. She rested her open laptop on her thigh, the screen tilted down at an angle making her uncomfortable. Her clenched fist was mushed into her check, and her elbow dug into her knees as she glared at the screen. Another rejection letter from a magazine refusing to publish her work. No one accepted the tale of the forty-foot albino *Carcharodon carcharias*; not even the tabloid newspapers would bite. No one ever recovered any evidence substantiating that the creature even existed. There were no reports of any sighting of the great white shark in over two months now. Kate wasn't able to find any evidence of the destruction it had wrought. The official cause of the sinking of the CCGS *Heart's Content* recorded by government officials was that it ran up against an outcrop of rock nearby and damaged the engine. They also revealed it to be the same location that Jonah McGilvery ran into when he sank the *Swift Current*. All the lives lost at sea that day were linked to the hallucination of a mysterious creature emerging from the abyss. Collective post-traumatic stress disorder developed amongst the survivors, and the true explanation of their deaths was never disclosed to the public, just the delusion left to blame in order to cope with the overwhelming catastrophe.

Labyrinth Oil had made billions of dollars since they began draining the oil out of the Grand Banks. The corporation also discovered plutonium underneath, but Kate's gut feeling led her to expect that they knew about it before they announced their pipeline. Kate discovered that Mr. Kurosawa had paid off the media to cover up the true tragedy. With no more sightings of any great white sharks along the coasts of Newfoundland, the breaking news of the discovery of plutonium caught the nation's attention. This made it easy for the media to make it seem like the only reason the sharks caught on the evening news was an anomaly. They believed the only reason they gathered off the shore in the first place was the dead humpback whale. They were drawn into Newfoundlands' shores during their journey back towards Africa from Nova Scotia. Kate tried to use her position at the university to warn people about the giant monstrosity, but her colleagues ridiculed her, discrediting all of her work she had produced trying to prove the albino abomination actually existed.

She sat alone in the airport, waiting for a departure to Alert in Nunavut, the northernmost settlement with a permanent population year-round. She resigned from the university in St. John's after they declined to fund her exploration into the shark. Unable to find anyone willing to pay for the frivolous expedition, her only chance of finding clues to the genetic mutation would be found from working at the research facility located in Alert. The military was conducting experiments with deep-submergence vehicles underneath the Arctic ice cap. She knew if there was any evidence of the albino predator it would be found somewhere in the vastly unexplored Arctic Ocean. She couldn't let all those people die in vain, to let people think that these people simply disappeared with no explanation. She owed it to Andy to prove that *Carcharodon carcharias* was still evolving, growing much larger to adjust to the earth's ocean's declining temperatures. Soon the *Carcharodon carcharias* would evolve into the world's most destructive predator. *Carcharocles megalodon* roamed the oceans before the last ice age and would soon be brought back into existence, but this time they would be prepared to survive the impending ice age.

AFTERWORD

I hope you enjoyed reading Carcharodon, but I am not an expert in the field. Any errors you find in this story are mine, and mine alone. Sometimes, I changed certain facts slightly to suit my needs to tell a better story. Other times, it's so far from the truth that it doesn't resemble the truth at all, and I'm sure you know which parts I'm talking about. They were meant to be fun and horrifying.

One thing I know is that sharks have always been a vitally necessary part of our ocean and that this story is not meant to demonize the species, it is simply a story I wrote for your enjoyment. You may find facts about sharks you didn't know in this book, you may even learn something useful from it.

However, in the end, this a fictional story. Sharks do not seek humans as prey. This animal is much older than we are and is much more successful in its habitat and a vital part of the equation that keeps a balance in the sea. If we can't learn to co-exist with them, then we may extinguish them from the face of the planet. We will always have a fear of sharks, they can be terrifying creatures under the right circumstances, and I exploited that deep ingrained fear for the purpose of writing this story. If you take anything away from reading this, is that we need to have a healthy respect for these beautiful creatures.

Now with that out of my system, I need to thank the people that helped me along the way. As always, I must give thanks to my beautiful wife, not only for marrying me, but for allowing me to write. It takes a lot of time and effort to put together a novel, and you always support me. To my kids, thanks for sleeping so I can get some writing done. I will also thank my mom and dad again. Your support means a lot to me. To my sister and brother-in-law, thanks for always promoting my book to everyone you know and bragging about me. This was the last novel I wrote while living in Newfoundland, but not to worry, I've continued to write stories about the shores of The Rock. Thanks to all of the members of my family for your support.

A huge thanks to Brad Dunne for agreeing to edit this novel after having taken on *Zombies on the Rock: The Republic of Newfoundland*. If it wasn't for you, I'd be up a certain creek without a paddle. Your keen eye and attention to detail made this novel so much better, and I'm eternally grateful for your time and advice. To Ellen, who designed this beautiful cover, it's my favourite and I couldn't have asked for better. To Matthew, for everything you do to help me along the way, I can't thank you enough. I would also like to thank all the members of the Engen Team who have helped make it easier getting noticed as a fiction author from Newfoundland by writing amazing fiction and capturing everyone's attention. Keep it up, it's amazing. I saved the best for last. That's right, you the reader. Thank you for purchasing this book. Without you, I'd be another Newfoundlander telling a tall tale at a kitchen party somewhere.

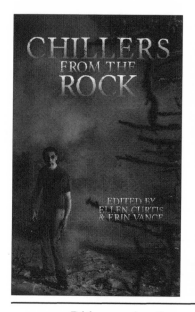 

Did you enjoy the work of Paul Carberry?
Read his other short fiction in Engen's bestselling anthologies,
including *Terror Nova*, *Chillers from the Rock*, *Fantasy from
the Rock*, *Flights from the Rock* and *From the Rock Stars*.

The From the Rock series features short stories written by a
diverse mix of the best authors in Canada, including award-
winning veterans of their craft, and brand new talent.

Also featuring the work of Ali House (*The Segment Delta
Archives*), Matthew LeDrew (*Coral Beach Casefiles, The
Xander Drew series*), Jon Dobbin (*The Starving*), and more!

These collections showcases the talent, imagination, and
prestige that Canada has to offer. From stories of censorship
gone awry to sentient buses, global warming to corporate-
branded culture, these collections have it all!

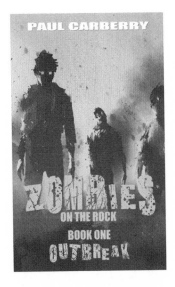

Zombies have taken over!
#1 Bestseller!

Zombie hordes created by the evil Pharmakon company have taken over the world, including the one place that always thought it was safe from the calamities of the outside: the quiet, scenic shores of Newfoundland's west coast. In this horrifying first volume, the island of Newfoundland is besieged by zombies and are left unprepared for the massacres that follow, struggling to stay alive as the city of Corner Brook falls to the undead hordes...

Book One: Outbreak (Feb 2017)
Book Two: The Viking Trail (Dec 2017)
Book Thee: Republic of Newfoundland (Sept 2019)

"[Carberry] draws in his readers from the first page, effortlessly providing the tension and fear necessary to create his terrifying apocalyptic tale."
— *Fiona Cooke Hogan, author of What Happened In Dingle*

"This is an astonishing first novel from Paul Carberry. I read it over the course of two days, and in those two days my time was divided thusly: reading it, and wishing I were still reading it."
— *Matthew LeDrew, author of Black Womb*

ABOUT THE AUTHOR

Paul Carberry is a huge proponent of the horror genre and its place in literature. He has two children, daughter Dana and son Rick, with his wife Leah.

Paul has published four novels with Engen Books: the *Zombies on the Rock* series, including to date: *Outbreak, The Viking Trail, The Republic of Newfoundland*, and, *Carcharodon*. He has also had numerous short stories featured in publication in anthologies such as *From the Rock* and *Terror Nova*, including The Light of Cabot Tower, Into the Forest, and Halloween Mummers.

His fifth novel, the fourth in his *Zombies on the Rock* franchise, will be released in 2021.